DRIFTWOOD

STORIES WASHED ASHORE

BEETASHOK CHATTERJEE

Readomania

Readomania Publishing
A division of Kurious Kind Media Private Limited
908, Vishwadeep Building, District Centre, Janakpuri,
New Delhi – 110058
books.readomania.com
email: contact@readomania.com
Facebook: facebook.com/iamreadomania
Twitter: twitter.com/iamreadomania
Instagram: iamreadomania

First Published in 2019 by Readomania

ISBN: 978-93-858547-7-4

Typeset in Palatino Linotype by Shine Graphics
Printed and bound at Thomson Press India Ltd.

Readomania

India has traditionally been the land of storytellers and a lot of us have an inherent skill of creating good plots, good stories and good narrations. With a little encouragement and support, many more authors will be widely read and attain a place in the sun. This is the essence of *Readomania*—an initiative that nurtures emerging stars of the literary world.

It would not be an exaggeration to say that *Readomania* is the talent hunt in fiction. It goes a step beyond by not just identifying the talent but also nurturing it and showcasing it to the world. In the process, we have created a powerhouse of content.

Readomania has four principal interest areas—traditional print publishing, online library of short stories and poetry, literary events and products.

The print publishing works towards delivering good quality content to the readers. We publish good authors in meaningful anthologies, novels and works of narrative non-fiction. Our books stand out for their perspectives, the plots, the language and most importantly their ability to enrich lives.

Take a break, read something nice, write something beautiful. Read our books or visit us at www.readomania.com and enjoy a whole new world of literature.

Dedicated to seafarers the world over, and to those who love the sea.

Contents

Foreword

Have you tried to look for modern sea stories at your local bookstores? Believe me, I have. I did not find any. After *Moby Dick, The Caine Mutiny* and *Lord Jim*—what? Those were written a long, long time ago. There was one called *The Black Tide* by Hammond Innes written in the early 80s which I thought was pretty good. After that, zilch. Nothing, as far as I know.

That got me thinking a couple of years ago. Why not a collection of sea stories that would appeal to landlubbers as well? On long voyages at sea, I had both time and the inclination. The idea was born, given shape and the keyboard of my laptop got busy.

And now, here we are.

Dear Reader, these are stories of the sea and of modern seafarers but not necessarily for seafarers alone. They are for anybody and everybody who likes to read fiction—tales of adventure, love, romance, piracy, intrigue...and human nature. They are for those who want to read a *ripping good yarn,* as sailors used to say once upon a time.

I am a seaman, someone who has spent his entire adult life at sea. That would mean more than forty years on the waves. Are these the stories of my experiences? Possibly. Are these stories based on the tales I have heard? Maybe. The truth is that they are all a seamless blend of fact and fiction, and even I do not remember where one ends and the other begins. But these are not tall tales or sailor's BS—all the events and experiences narrated could and probably did happen to some modern seafarer somewhere at some point of time.

These stories are to give you a glimpse of sea life. I want you to feel what it is like to be at sea; to empathise with the trials and tribulations of a seaman. I hope, dear Reader, by the time you finish this collection (and I hope you don't abandon ship midway!), you have caught that glimpse.

CAPT. BEETASHOK CHATTERJEE
New Delhi
June 2019

1

The Piano Man

It felt good to step on land again. Anand stamped his feet hard on the ground to be doubly sure and raised a small cloud of dust in the process. The reddish-brown dust of bauxite lay everywhere along the jetty like a threadbare carpet. He hurried on towards the dock gates to catch the bus to town. He had just a few hours of free time and was determined to spend them as far away from the ship as possible.

It was a hot, sunny afternoon in the port of Gove in Australia's Northern Territory. Anand's ship had docked that morning. Alcan Gove, the mining company that ran the port for its exports had a bus service to town, as a friendly gesture to the seafarers who wanted to go ashore during their off-duty hours. Australia is like that. One of the few countries in the world that still gives a damn about seafarers who visit her shores. Anand had no company to go ashore with, but he did not really mind. A lone wolf by nature, he had always been comfortable in his solitude.

The hot, dry wind blew dust in through the window of the bus and tugged at his hair and shirt. His lips turned chapped and dry. He put on his dark glasses to keep out the glare of the harsh, bright light of the day. All he could see outside his window was a broken waste of desert—the desolate, rugged Australian Outback. And the road ahead, straight and narrow, heading into infinity. In the distance the road evaporated into mirage after vaporous mirage, each only to disappear as the bus came closer.

After about half an hour's drive, they reached the town of Gove. Three dusty dock workers and the solitary Indian seaman got off the bus. The bus driver told Anand to be at the same spot at 5.30 pm for the return trip. They all gave a friendly wave of thanks to the bus driver who turned and drove away. The three locals walked away in earnest conversation and Anand was left alone. He stood on the sidewalk and looked around.

He felt like he was in one of the old Hollywood westerns in which the tall, laconic stranger walks into a sleepy, little ghost town as silent eyes watch him from doorways, porches and balconies of rotting houses, where the doors hang precariously on their hinges and groan in pain with every gust of dry wind. But no, he chuckled to himself, he mustn't let his imagination carry him away. This was a small town, but quite a pretty, well-maintained, modern one. And there really didn't seem to be anyone around to watch him on that blazing afternoon.

He stood there for a while, deciding what to do next. More than anything else, he wanted a chilled beer or two, then a local meal and some Internet time. Perhaps later he would also browse around the few shops that seemed to be open. He needed to head back by 5.30, so there really wasn't that much time to do other stuff. As he started to walk down the main street, he noticed the familiar signs of a McDonald's and a KFC. But no, he wanted something different to eat. And a tall chilled glass of Foster's. Or two.

The faint sound of a piano made him stop outside a pub. '*Eddie's*', the sign beckoned. There was somebody playing inside for sure. It wasn't a recording; somebody inside was practising a tune. Anand walked in through the wooden swing doors. Inside, a glass door automatically slid open to receive him with a cool blast of air conditioning. He stepped in, stood for an instant at the entrance to let his eyes adjust to the dark and then walked in. The place was empty. The décor was Wild West, with the bar counter on the right and a piano on the left. There was an elderly gent sitting on the piano stool, practising a few notes on the keys and a sullen, tired-looking, middle-aged woman in an apron sitting by the bar examining her fingernails. No customers.

They both turned to look at the visitor. The old gent smiled and nodded in greeting. The woman slowly got off the bar stool to fetch a menu card.

Anand took a seat facing the piano and nodded back to the pianist. The older man got up and walked over. He was tall and thin. Twinkling eyes framed by thick grey eyebrows, stubbled cheeks sunk in. Grey hair escaped from the baseball cap on his head in several directions.

'Hi, I'm Bill,' he said. The voice was hoarse. They shook hands. 'You from the ship, mate?' Anand nodded. Bill sat down opposite him. 'Where's home?' he asked.

'New Delhi, India.'

'Aha... India! I thought as much, son. Mary!' he called out to the woman who was approaching them with a menu card. 'This lad is from India!' The woman gave the visitor a stiff smile as if she couldn't care less, said nothing and waited for Anand to decide on his order. She was an unattractive, sullen specimen. Her forehead was wrinkled by years of consistent scowling, and her countenance seemed drained of any signs of joy or amusement.

Anand placed his order along with a beer. Realising that the old man was in no hurry to leave his table, he ordered a beer for him as well, out of politeness, and received a nod of appreciation. Mary walked away and returned with two tall chilled glasses of Foster's. Just what he needed. Apparently, the old man needed it as much.

'That's my wife,' Bill said, after a long swig. 'Doesn't talk much, does she?' he added after making sure she was out of earshot.

'So do you own this place, Bill?'

'No, son, no such luck. We just work here,' Bill said, taking another sip of his beer. 'You know, we're from India too. Born and raised in Calcutta.'

'What! How come?'

'Yes! We're AIs, son... Anglo Indians. Moved here twenty years ago.'

On scrutinising Bill's features, Anand realised that it could be true. There were so many AIs who could pass off as Caucasians. Anand had heard of the mass exodus of AIs from all parts of India to Australia and the UK in the 60s, 70s and 80s to seek greener pastures, hoping that they would blend in better with the local populace and be accepted. Except that most of the youngsters who left India with dreams in their hearts and holes in their pockets never studied enough or acquired any qualification to get a real good start in their new environs. Just hoped to get by on their looks and charm. Didn't work for most of them. Here was a shining example, Anand thought, but wisely kept his opinion to himself.

He found the older man looking at him thoughtfully. Experience seemed to dance on Bill's lips like a curious child. Anand could tell that this old man had stories to tell, and was dying to find a willing audience. He did not have to wait that long. 'Since you're a seaman, mate, I want to tell you a story that happened to a friend of mine,' Bill said. 'He was a Captain.'

'I am listening,' Anand said, sipping his beer. He welcomed it; he had an hour to kill.

'Well, son, this happened in the late 80s,' Bill began his story, leaning back in his chair. 'My friend was Captain on a small bulk carrier docked in the port of Mombasa in east Africa. They'd been in port for two weeks discharging their cargo. You know two weeks is a long time to be in port.

Anything can happen.' Anand nodded in agreement. He did not like long stays in port either. The daily shipboard routine got disrupted, routine maintenance suffered and the ship became dirty and messy with so many dock workers boarding and leaving in shifts day after day. Chaotic would be an apt word.

'Anyway, they finally sailed from Mombasa and headed south,' clearing his throat, Bill continued. 'A day later, the crew spotted two stowaways hiding in the Steering Gear Compartment aft! Yes, two young, skinny black boys lying on coils of rope, scared shitless.' He took a long swig of his beer. 'The Bosun hauled these two boys up to the Captain. The Captain asked them a lot of questions but they spoke no English. They had no identity papers with them…nothing.

'Now the Captain was in a dilemma. What was he to do with these bloody stowaways? He was stuck with them forever! They had no papers with them, so no country was going to accept them. And if these boys escaped in some foreign port, the Captain would be held responsible. He was not only stuck with them, he also had to make sure they were looked after and that they did not escape. Between the devil and the deep sea, mate! So you can imagine what all was going through my friend's mind. He needed time to think.

'So he ordered the two stowaways to be locked up in the Paint Locker among the drums of paint while he decided on his next course of action. He gave them three meals a day, or so he told me, and allowed them to come out for an hour or so to get fresh air. Not exactly the Hilton, eh? He did not report these stowaways to his office, or to any authority. Because he knew that the shit would hit the fan, pardon my French, mate. He'd get blamed for allowing the stowaways to come on board in the first place. So a lot was going through my friend's mind. Then after two days of sailing he came to a decision.'

Anand, seeing that both glasses were empty, ordered another round. He was enjoying the story but was wondering where this was going. It crossed Anand's mind that Bill too may have been a seafarer once, since he seemed to know ships. Or maybe Bill's friend had related his adventures to him in painstaking detail.

Bill was warming up to his tale. 'They were passing Durban, I think, when the Captain headed closer to the shore, stopped the ship, ordered the two stowaways to be put in a 200 litre drum each, along with some food and water and cast them adrift in the sea. Yes, the boys did protest but a couple of good, hard whacks from the burly Bosun took care of that.'

Anand thought he hadn't heard clearly. 'What did you say?'

'You heard me, son. That's what he did. That's what he thought was the best course of action at that time. He didn't want to get into trouble with his employer or with any port authority for having stowaways on board. That would have been bad news for all concerned. He didn't want to get stuck with them forever, because he knew no country would accept them without papers. He figured that they would be picked up by some passing ship on the coast, mistaken as refugees and then taken to the next port or wherever. Then it wouldn't be *his* problem. He wanted to get rid of *his* problem, and the sooner the better. But he was sure they'd survive.'

'How could he have been so sure they'd survive?' Anand asked incredulously. 'Come on! Two boys in empty drums at the mercy of the sea and sharks! Suppose no ship spotted them? Suppose they drifted seaward, into the Indian Ocean, never to be found? How was that Captain so sure they'd be rescued?'

Bill shrugged his shoulders, as if to say it wasn't his fault, and was silent for a while. Mary came over, served the fish and chips Anand had ordered and walked away. The seaman muttered his thanks and started eating, deep in thought. 'So what happened next, Bill?' he asked between mouthfuls.

The old man took a swig from his glass and resumed, 'The ship rounded the Cape of Good Hope and her next port of call was Cape Town. On arrival, she stayed at anchor for about a week before going to the berth, as there was none available. When she finally docked, the Coast Guard boarded the vessel. The Captain thought it was for a routine inspection. But no, it wasn't, mate. They first took a round on deck and examined the Paint Locker in particular. They then went up to the bridge and asked to see the navigation charts for the voyage from the last port of call. Sure enough, off Durban, they noted from the positions plotted that the ship had come closer to the shore and then moved away again. The time notations were also there along with the positions. That seemed to confirm what the Coast Guard already knew.

'The Captain was arrested on charges of attempted manslaughter.'

Bill paused and watched the seaman silently while Anand digested this piece of information. 'But how…?'

'The two stowaways survived, mate!' Bill exclaimed, slapping his thigh. 'They were washed ashore and taken to the nearest port authority. I guess they were able to name the ship and describe the contents of the Paint Locker well too. They must have also given the authorities the time and date when they had been cast adrift. Those timings must've matched the chart information.'

Anand nodded with satisfaction. There was a God in Heaven after all. He scooped up the remnants on his plate into his mouth and chewed slowly, waiting for Bill to continue. Mary was back perched on her bar stool, not saying a word, ignoring the two men.

'The ship was Norwegian flagged. So Norwegian law applied. After the initial inquiry on board where everybody's statements were taken, the Captain was taken to Oslo. He stood trial over there. Poor bugger didn't have a chance. He was sentenced to jail for two years.'

Anand pushed his plate away and washed down his food with the beer. He waited, sensing that the story was not over yet.

Bill paused again, watching him, apparently reading his mind. He let out a sigh and continued, 'Did you know his wife was on board with him at that time? She was devastated. Didn't have a clue to all that was going on under her nose. She had to make her own way back home to India in disgrace. To Calcutta.' He turned to call to his wife. 'Isn't that right, Mary?' She glared at him and said nothing.

Anand stared at him uncomprehendingly and then at the woman. It then dawned on him.

Bill smiled ruefully and nodded. 'You got it, son. It is *my* story.'

Anand was at a loss for words. He felt the air in the room was laden with sadness and regret, as if a rain cloud had entered and was hovering over him.

'I ruined my life and hers with that mistake. Life was never the same again. I believe there was a story in the

Indian papers about this. Before your time, son. The word got around that I was in jail in some foreign land. My family was ostracised by our own community back home. We were reduced to penury. There was nothing I could do from jail to help them. When I was released two years later, I was broken in body and spirit. No shipping company wanted to employ me. I was a disgrace. My licence was revoked.

'To add insult to injury…my son, then in his teens, developed a form of muscular dystrophy. There was no cure for this. He died a few years later. Divine retribution, mate. Divine retribution. That is when we moved here to Australia.

'I play the piano and help out behind the bar when there are customers. Mary waits at tables. And so life goes on. No worries mate!' His cheerful remark belied the sadness in his eyes and smile.

The piano man stood up and walked up to the piano. He sat down and began to play a slow, sad tune, the sound of music filling the room like a tide rushing in.

It was time to leave, though a part of him wanted to stay on and offer solace to this elderly couple.

But Anand remembered he had a couple of things to do in town before the bus came to pick him up. He paid his bill, left a hefty tip and stood up to go. He shook hands with the couple and left in a sombre mood, shaken by the story. How one mistake can ruin several lives, he reflected as he stepped out into the harsh light of the late afternoon sun. The door swung shut behind him.

The old man continued to sit and play for a minute or two watching the door, then walked up to the table and pocketed the money left behind by yet another naïve and sentimental seafarer. He strutted up to the woman, put his arm around her shoulder and chuckled. 'Fell for it hook, line and sinker, didn't he, love? I love these sailors!'

'You and your stories, man! But they keep getting better 'n' better!' The woman retorted, her sour features breaking into a grin, revealing a missing tooth, as she deftly reached out and took the money from the old man's pocket to tuck inside her blouse, before pushing him away.

2

Sapphire Blue

My friend Paul loves the sea. A bit baffling, because he quit his job in the Coast Guard to follow his passion for music. No regrets there. But he hasn't got over his love for the sea.

Have you ever looked at the sea on a clear sunny day in the middle of the morning? It is sapphire blue when calm… blue like the gemstone…and it smiles and twinkles in the light. He generally chooses this time of day to come to the beach and walk on the white sand. Today is no different. The waves on the rising tide gently lap around his feet and ankles as he walks in a slow rhythm towards the cove a mile away. Left, right, left, right…his footprints on the wet sand get erased behind him by the tide as he walks on. He quite likes that. For that is the kind of person Paul is. Wants his footprints on the sands of time to be washed away…he likes to move on, never look back.

There is the breeze in his hair and a song on his lips. 'Blue sky, blue sea, blue me!' he says out loud in a singsong way, looking at his beloved sea. Eh? Where did that line come from? Blue sky, blue sea, blue me? It makes him chuckle to himself. Maybe a new poem or a song in the offing? He makes a mental note.

He espies a distant figure sitting on the rocks. She has been waiting for him at the cove. She keeps on looking at him as he approaches her. Her blue eyes…yes, they are sapphire blue too, like the sea today…are worried. Her lips are slightly parted, revealing perfect teeth. Very desirable. She looks tense, a little wound up. She is dying to tell him something, dying to get it off her chest. Knowing her, he's pretty sure that what she is going to tell him will not be pleasant to hear.

'What took you so long?' Maria's Mediterranean accent is charming. 'I've been waiting a long time, you know.'

He gives her a perfunctory kiss and sits down on the rock beside her. 'Sorry, darling,' he says, not meaning it at all. 'How *are* you?'

'It is done,' she says, her eyes searching his countenance for a reaction.

Paul looks at her. Brown ringlets frame a tanned, freckled face. Deep blue eyes, apprehensive and a little scared. A small, lithe body under the white cotton skirt and top...a body that he is familiar with under the sheets and has grown to love. He says nothing, waiting for her to continue.

'Potassium chloride injection. Injected in the navel. Pathologists never look there. It does not leave traces,' she comments. Her blue eyes are steady, holding his gaze. 'Heart stopped.'

A woman of few words, his Maria.

'I had been a nurse in my native Sicily,' she adds. He nods knowingly. Yes, she had told him her life history. Maria had come to the States three years ago looking for a better life. She had found work in Florida working as a private nurse for elderly people. They had met at this very beach a year ago. She loved the sea and sand as much as he did, and they took long walks together on this beach. They had gradually got to know each other well. Very well, in fact.

They sit there for a while looking seaward. He doesn't know what to say. A distant ship on the horizon takes a long time to go out of sight. She has just spoken to him of having murdered somebody, and he allows that piece of information to sink in. Why she has done it, he doesn't know. Why she is confessing to him, he doesn't know. What she expects him to do about it, he doesn't know.

Finally, she gets up, dusts her skirt with the back of her hand, bends down to kiss his cheek and walks away. He keeps looking out to sea.

He ruminates for a while over where his life is heading and what to do next. He hasn't found the answers to his questions yet. Even Harvey, the only friend he confides in other than me, hasn't been much of a help, notwithstanding his good intentions. With a sigh, he gets up to head home. But he stops by at the supermarket to pick up groceries first.

There is a joyous bark behind the front door as he lets himself in. That would be Toffee, their Golden Labrador, and the happiest dog in the world. He smiles—it is always good to be back home, even if it is only from a walk on the beach a few miles away, and be welcomed warmly. Even if only by a dog.

Tracy is in the back garden attending to her plants. She turns and flashes him a smile. 'Back already? It must be lunchtime then!' She walks past him inside. Her brown curly hair is tied up in a ponytail. She walks to the kitchen and he watches her slim perfection till she is out of sight around the corner. A Scorpio sphinx in a calico dress.

'*Aw shucks*!' The exclamation mark is loud and long, followed by a '*Jeesus*!'. You can take a Texan out of Texas, but you cannot take Texas out of a Texan. Tracy will always remain a Houston girl with that endearing drawl, no matter where she stays. He is guessing she has burnt the roast again while daydreaming or getting distracted or whatever she does so well, and he chuckles. Fortunately no hunger pains are gnawing at his stomach and he doesn't feel annoyed. He has learnt to be patient with his harum-scarum wife.

They sit down for a hastily prepared meal of baked beans and toast with chilled orange juice from the fridge. 'So how was your day, hon?' Tracy has recovered from her dismay at ruining lunch and is back to her distracted self. 'Went to the beach as usual?'

He nods. He doesn't tell her who he met there, nor does she ask.

She is soon lost in her own world again. Her blue eyes are gazing into the distance; her tanned, freckled face is solemn, as she eats and waits for him to say something.

What do you want me to say, darling? He asks her silently. *That I can't live with you but can't live without you? That I love you to death and yet wish I'd never met you? That I can't sleep at night wondering if I should leave you or not? That I wish for a miracle to take place and sort my life out?*

'I'm working on a new song,' he says instead, between gulps of orange juice. 'About the sea. It was really beautiful out there today.'

'Hmmm...' she is only half listening, already daydreaming again about God-knows-what. She does that a lot. They were married six years ago in Los Angeles. He was a young Warrant Officer in the United States Coast Guard then, dying to follow his dream of becoming a songwriter. There were so many tunes and lyrics swirling in his head always he knew back then that this was his calling. Tracy, trying to make it as an actress, urged him to quit and follow his dreams. He owes this to her. Without her support, he would still be languishing as a Chief Petty Officer or something like that in the USCG, visiting ships in port as part of Port Security and bullying the foreign crews of third world countries. That is how I met him, by the way. But that is another story.

By the time they moved here to Florida, she had given up her career ambition and settled into domesticity. He wonders sometimes if she misses showbiz, but she never speaks of it. This is a relief, and absolves him of any momentary twinges of guilt. He finds her bright and musically talented too. She helps him with his work sometimes, with a line here and a tune there when he gets stuck in the middle of a composition.

A wet nose sniffs at his ankles. Toffee whines and licks Paul's bare, hairy leg. He tickles him under his chin and strokes his head. Satisfied, Toffee goes over to his mistress and flops down at her feet. His devotion to her is unconditional. The way Paul's should be.

Lunch over, Paul clears up and steps out onto the front lawn. Tracy returns to the back garden. The rest of the day stretches out in front of him, not a minute of it filled. He should be stepping into his studio in the basement to work on a new song, he tells himself reluctantly. But he does not have a deadline to meet, he has the Florida sun glowing orange on his eyelids and a pretty home a short drive away from the Fort Lauderdale Riverwalk. He counts his blessings. It isn't such a bad life being a successful songwriter, that too in a country with the largest entertainment business in the world; he could have done worse. Like remain in the United States Coast Guard. He whistles for Toffee to come out and join him. Unfortunately, Toffee's filial loyalty to Tracy is not to be questioned and the dog has already joined her in the back garden.

There is a call Paul makes before he decides what to do next. To his friend Harvey.

'Hi, Harv! Are we on for tomorrow morning?'

'Sure, Paul. How about nine?'

'Great. See you tomorrow.'

He makes an effort to shake off his lethargy and decides to work on a new song while the words are still forming in his head. Going down to his basement studio, he switches on the dim lights and the AC, sits down at his piano and starts tinkering with the keys. In his mind's eye, he sees the sapphire-like blue sea of the morning in front of him as he tries out a few chords on the piano. Words and tunes run amok in his head as he struggles with the genesis of a new song. The anger and despair welling up once again inside him cause him to thump the keys with a vengeance, creating loud discordant notes. But he carries on.

It is around 5 pm when he decides to pack up for the day. He has a verse complete and a tune to go along with it…well, sort of. It still needs to be fine-tuned, pun not intended. He feels better after a day's work doing what he does best. He goes up to the living room and calls out. There is a silence. Tracy has gone out. He calls for Toffee. The dog isn't home either. Oh well….

He feels the need to clear his head, and heads for the Riverwalk downtown. He parks the car a good distance away in the parking lot and walks on foot to join the melee. As usual, the place is vibrant, full of life. People of all ages walking, cycling, and skateboarding…the weekend crowd is swelling. Tourists in shorts and sandals drifting along, apparently going nowhere. There are people thronging the ice-cream stalls. There are people waiting to rent kayaks on the river. There is a group doing yoga further on. He is passing the Dog Training Classes, when he hears someone call his name.

'Hello, Paul!' He turns to see who is calling him.

It is Annie Walker. She is getting her dog trained to sit up and beg. She is an attractive, friendly woman, but today he doesn't feel up to stopping and conversing. He just wants to move on and mingle with the crowd, absorbing the sights and sounds of his surroundings. But no, Annie wants to talk and walks up to him.

'So what are you doing here, Paul? Good to see you!' A pronounced New York accent.

'Ummm...nothing much, Annie. Just clearing my head. How're you doing?'

'I'm just here for the buzz too, Paul,' she says with a laugh, revealing perfect teeth in a tanned, freckled face. Her deep blue eyes are alight with *joie de vivre*. 'Look, Biscuit loves it too. Just watch him flirting!' True, her handsome Golden Labrador is getting a lot of attention from the canines around him and enjoying himself, too busy to notice Paul.

He has met Annie a few times here and there. At the bowling alley, the supermarket and sometimes even in his own neighbourhood—walking the dog or shopping or jogging. They are not friends yet, more like acquaintances. But she is slim, attractive, friendly and always pleasant. And she seems to like him. Nothing more. She'd told him once that her husband was a Wall Street stockbroker, and that they are now divorced. However, that setback does not seem to deter her from enjoying her life. He too is wary of getting more involved. This casual friendship suits him fine.

He chats with her for a while and then bids her goodbye, moving further on into the crowd. He needs to be alone right now, clear his thoughts. He tries not to brood over his problems, and to distract himself he finds a convenient place to sit and look at people passing by. It is only after an hour or so that he goes back to his car and heads home. Tracy is back, watching a sitcom on TV and nursing a glass of wine, Toffee lazing at her feet. He joins her for the remainder of a pleasant evening at home.

He doesn't tell her who he met at Riverwalk, nor does she ask.

Next morning he goes to visit his friend Harvey at his office downtown. The shining nameplate outside Harvey's fifteenth floor office says 'Harvey Feldstein, M.D.' with a smaller inscription that says 'Psychiatrist'. Harvey and he were in college together. Despite their disparate professions, they remain friends. Harvey ushers him into his inner office and gets him a cup of coffee. They exchange pleasantries and discuss football before getting down to brass tacks.

'There doesn't seem to be any improvement in her condition, Harvey,' he says, 'What is your assessment since you last saw her?'

'Not so good. It'll take time, Paul. I do admit it's taking longer than I expected.'

'How long, Harv? *Months? Years?*' Paul's voice rises in frustration.

Harvey pretends not to notice and shrugs non-committally. 'Can't say, Paul. It is MPD—Multiple Personality Disorder. Or DID—Dissociative Identity Disorder—as it's called nowadays. Your wife has several identities—three that you know of—but there could be more. All of these personalities are unaware of each other.

'Tracy doesn't know that Maria exists. Nor does she have any clue about Annie. Her mind picks up identities of ordinary people and she becomes those people. Randomly.

Remember she was an actress? That helps too with her role playing and the accents. Her lapses in attention, her distracted demeanour, her daydreaming…these are classic symptoms of MPD, Paul. There must've been some trauma in her childhood which she is still reluctant to reveal. She's holding back too much.'

The silence stretches out, filling the space between them.

Finally Paul breaks it, 'So what happens to me, Harv? How long can I go on like this? How long can I stop myself from shaking or slapping or, worse, strangling Maria or Annie or whoever Tracy may turn into tomorrow to tell them to wake the hell up? Maria told me yesterday that she's killed somebody. Could it possibly be true? God! I love my wife, Harv, but I can't go on like this.'

'You must, Paul,' Harvey said quietly, 'for Tracy's sake. I know you love her very much. I'm giving it my best shot. Let's hope for the best. You've got to have hope!'

The discussion goes on for some time. Finally, a despondent Paul takes his leave and heads for the beach. It is time for his daily stroll. Another bright, sunny day. The sea is sapphire blue like yesterday. He wonders with some dread if Maria will be there waiting for him. With another horrific confession.

He wonders what life has in store for him, where it will take him next. Another day of wondering, thinking, not losing hope and making plans for the future. But as he starts his slow, rhythmic walk on the white sand, I want to remind him of a line some cynic told me once, 'If you want to make God laugh, my friend, tell Him you've got plans!'

3

Goldilocks and the Three Bears

'W*hat the f...?'*

The loud, rapid knocking on the door was incessant, shattering his alcohol-induced slumber. Tony Fernandes looked at the clock by his bedside with red, bleary eyes. It was 2.30 am.

'This had better be good,' he muttered to himself, as he wrapped a towel around his nakedness, determined that whoever was outside that door would pay for it.

He stumbled out of his bedroom to the Day Room cabin door, unlocked and opened it. It was Khan, the Second Mate on duty, looking worried. No, having a panic attack would be a more apt description. Khan was sweating and breathing heavily.

There were three women standing behind him. Tony blinked again to focus, rubbing his eyelids. Yes, three... women! Two were middle-aged and black, dressed garishly in tight fitting clothes, bosoms popping out of their low-cut, sleeveless tops, and wearing knee-length boots. The third was a young, chubby white blonde with wavy golden hair up to her shoulders. She was dressed a little more conservatively in a white top and red corduroy pants.

Tony glared at Khan. 'Couldn't you call first?' But Khan did not answer. His distraught expression said it all—he obviously needed help.

When he looked again at the women, he realised what was wrong. The blonde was crying and her clothes were spattered with blood. Her left wrist had a deep gash in it. She was gripping it tightly with her right hand to stop the blood from oozing out, and straining to hold back tears of pain.

Goldilocks.

That was the name that immediately sprung to his mind. The two older women stood impassively, their facial expressions revealing nothing, their dull eyes telling him that they had seen a lot worse.

'Holy shit!' Tony muttered, the first expletive that crossed his mind. Being the Chief Mate of the ship and the senior of the two, his help was undoubtedly needed. He nodded to Khan indicating he would be ready in no time to join them, shut the door and went in to wash his face and put on some clothes.

In a couple of minutes he was back outside his cabin, dressed and alert. For a while, they all stood and stared at each other. Then Tony motioned them all to follow him.

'Have you informed the Old Man?' Tony asked the younger officer, as he led the group down the lit corridor to the Officers' Recreation Room on the same deck. Khan shook his head. Tony grunted his approval. Some things were best kept secret from the Captain of that ship. The Old Man would undoubtedly raise a shrill hue and cry, conduct a long-winded inquiry and send a detailed report of the incident to the Head Office, who would retaliate by burying them in confessions and explanations. Paper work for nothing. Tony had a low opinion of paper tigers.

The Recreation Room was empty as expected at that hour. It was a fairly large carpeted room lined with sofas. There were two coffee tables widely spaced, with an entertainment centre comprising of a television set, audio system and a VCR on one wall. A bookcase to the side contained the ship's library of books, video and audio cassettes. Framed pictures of company vessels, including this one, adorned the laminated walls. In short, a typical Recreation Room found on hundreds of merchant ships worldwide.

'Get me the first aid kit from the hospital. Quickly!' Tony ordered the Second Mate, who left the room. He bid the rest of them to sit down. They all did, quietly.

The three women sat down heavily on the same sofa. The two older ones started muttering to each other in their own language, while Goldilocks sat in one corner of the sofa, huddled in pain, sobbing and bleeding quietly. Tony tried to understand what the two were saying, but it was the local Creole language, not even French, of which he had a working knowledge. After all, the ship, on that day in February of 1980, was docked at the port of Pointe Des Galets in the Indian Ocean island of Ile de Reunion. Access to ships in port was free and easy those days, especially in small ports like this one. People were free to visit ships in port, and seamen off duty were free to go ashore at any time. It was an era when there was no international security or paranoia against terrorism. The good old days....

They all waited. The clock ticked to the soft sobbing sounds of the young girl. Tony cursed under his breath, wondering what was keeping the Second Mate. The young girl's sobbing was bothering him. His heart went out to her, but he restrained himself from going across to her to put an arm around her or stroke her hair. He waited, tapping his fingers to a tune in his head.

Khan returned with the dressings finally. And, thoughtfully, cigarettes too. At Tony's nod, the young officer made the guests comfortable by putting on some soft music and offered them a cigarette each, which they accepted gratefully. After Khan lit Goldilocks' cigarette for her, Tony cleaned the gash on her plump, white wrist with antiseptic, covered it with cotton wool soaked in Dettol and slowly dressed her wound with bandage. Fortunately it looked like it didn't need stitches. Tears streamed down her pale cheeks. He was feeling a tenderness that he hadn't felt before, and he finally couldn't help but reach out to wipe her tears with his hand, muttering softly, 'Don't cry, don't cry'. Goldilocks looked at him with her teary, grey eyes and smiled her thanks.

'All okay, Chief?' A long-haired head popped in as the door opened.

It was John, the Able Bodied Seaman on duty or AB for short, causing Tony to curse under his breath Again.

'What do you want, John?'

'I was manning the gangway when these three…ahem… ladies boarded. They wanted to see the Officer on Duty. I called Sec down on my walkie-talkie radio immediately, and advised him to wake you up. I thought it's better you deal with the situation, Chief.'

Tony grunted in approval. John, being a more experienced seaman than Second Mate Khan, had given the young officer sound advice. It was quite a situation—three ladies of the night, one hurt and bleeding. Not something that happens often on a ship. He wished though that John hadn't been on duty. The flamboyant AB would spread the yarn, sprinkled with spice, to everybody on board by morning, with himself in the lead role.

'Why aren't you on duty at the gangway, John?'

'Fire rounds, Sir,' was the prompt reply, to which Tony had no rejoinder. He realised that John, bursting with curiosity, had tracked them down to the Officers' Recreation Room, determined to get a ringside seat to the drama.

A whitish cloud of cigarette smoke hung in the air as John entered uninvited, shutting the door behind him.

He ignored Tony's scowl. Then seeing that no one was paying him any attention, he announced, 'I'll get coffee for everybody!' without being asked, and left for the pantry.

Abba was playing on the stereo, one of their slow melodious numbers. The music and the cigarettes were having a soporific effect on the three women. They were visibly relaxing, though young Goldilocks still seemed to be in a little bit of pain. Khan slipped out back to the ship's hospital and brought two codeine phosphate tablets with a glass of water. Goldilocks nodded her thanks and popped both the pills. She leaned back and closed her eyes.

John was back in ten minutes with six steaming mugs of coffee. He passed a mug to each of them with a show of ceremony.

'Anything to get these women's attention,' Tony thought darkly.

The coffee was strong and black. Just what they seemed to need, as the women sipped and nodded their appreciation. Without as much as a by-your-leave, John too settled down on a single sofa with his mug. This annoyed Tony, but he masked it. He would deal with John later.

'Speak English?' Tony asked the three tentatively, taking charge again.

The blonde nodded. The other two older women made no acknowledgement, their hard eyes expressionless as they blew out smoke from their nostrils.

'What is your name?' Tony asked Goldilocks.

'Lily,' she replied. 'And this is Yolanda, and that one is Marie.' Yolanda and Marie nodded in greeting. The former was tall and statuesque like an ebony goddess, the latter lean and below average height. Both seemed to be in their late thirties.

'Tell us, Lily, what happened tonight.'

In halting, broken English Lily narrated her tale of woe to the three seafarers. Normally they came to the docks every night and boarded any ship that would allow them to board. Their 'manager' had an agreement with the security detail at the dock gates. Last evening, just before midnight, it was the ship behind theirs. Unfortunately, it hadn't been business as usual on that ship. They ran into a spot of trouble there. After having delivered her 'wares', Lily didn't get paid. She got into a scuffle with her customer, a belligerent, drunk Ukrainian seaman and the fight got ugly. When she almost scratched his eye out, he attacked her with a knife and slashed her wrist. The three of them just managed to escape from that ship and rushed to the nearest one for safety and urgent medical attention—theirs.

And there they were. Sitting with three long-haired, unshaven, scruffy men who themselves were not sure what to do next. The three seafarers were silent as they heard her story out, each of them occupied with his respective thoughts, all staring at the comely narrator.

A maelstrom of emotions was running through Tony's mind. What should he do now? What did he *want* to do next? What did they want to do next?

Here were three hookers sitting in front of him comfortably in scanty, tight clothing. Smoking and relaxed. Grateful and well-disposed towards him. Enticing cleavages for all to see. Ready to be taken in his arms and off to bed. Maybe a threesome, if he was persuasive enough. This was every seaman's fantasy! How often does one get a chance like that? And yet...he felt no desire. Not after seeing Lily clutching her wrist and holding back tears of pain. Not after seeing the spatter of blood on her clothes.

Goldilocks' condition had extinguished any desire that may have smouldered; he felt only tenderness and pity.

John wished he had some marijuana to offer Goldilocks. If only he'd known, he would have got some from the bar just outside the docks; he had met a dealer there on shore leave yesterday. Lily and he would smoke a joint together and it would really dull her pain. She could go to sleep in his arms and in his bed. Lust was fun, wasn't it? In the morning they would make love like it was their last day on earth. She could stay with him on board till the ship sailed a couple of days later. That would really make him a hero among his shipmates, the talk of the town. He winked at Goldilocks, who winced and looked away.

Young Khan felt his heart pumping hard and a faint stirring in his loins. He had never been this close to foreign women before. Any woman, for that matter. The way they were dressed—where did one get to see such sights back home? Bare shoulders, deep cleavage...he wanted to touch their skins, run his hand over their bodies. He wanted to kiss the blonde's pale skin; he wanted to see the tall black woman naked atop him. As the last image flashed through his mind, a rush of guilt accompanied the thought and Khan asked God fervently to forgive him for such blasphemy. In return he got a knowing smile from Yolanda, who seemed to guess what was going on in the blushing young man's mind. Marie too seemed to possess the power of telepathy, for she glanced at him and wiggled her tongue suggestively.

Nobody spoke till the coffee cups were empty and the last cigarette was stubbed out. The air was redolent with tobacco smoke. The two older women muttered something in Creole to the blonde. It was as if they were trying to persuade her to do something. Goldilocks looked at her three 'bears', her eyes imploring a message, but she seemed hesitant to speak.

Tony by then had made his decision what to do next. He stood up, switched off the music and spoke to his visitors, looking at Goldilocks in particular.

'Go home, Lily. You need to go home and rest,' he told them. 'You are in no condition to work. Go home.'

Goldilocks nodded, despondent. She spoke to her colleagues who shrugged non-committally.

A vexed John looked up at Tony questioningly. Why was the Chief letting go of this opportunity? Was he an idiot? Tony gave him a hard stare that brooked no argument. They all stood up slowly to leave, John the last. 'Company policy,' Khan added with a nervous laugh as an explanation to Goldilocks, who said nothing. He too was disappointed at the Chief Mate's decision, but knew better than to show dissent.

It was around 3.30 am by the time they all came down from the Officers' Deck to the gangway. They stood for an instant facing each other—three hirsute, dishevelled seamen of differing nationalities, facing one white French girl and two African women. A veritable United Nations conference. Then each man got a hug and a peck on the cheek from each visitor and stood by chivalrously as the 'ladies' gingerly walked down the gangway steps in their high-heeled boots. On reaching the jetty, they waved to their hosts, blew kisses, turned and walked ahead.

Dawn had yet to arrive. A full moon was setting in the west. John studied the silver glow of the moon briefly. In a couple of hours the first shift of longshoremen would enter the docks at daybreak and board the various ships in the harbour to begin the day's loading and unloading of cargo. The lights would be switched off on the docks and on all the ships in the port. The crew would scurry out on deck at the sound of the siren to open the ship's hatch covers and get ready the ship's derricks or cranes for another busy day in port.

Tony and his mates watched the three women walk away. The docks were well lit. They could see them clearly, walking slowly and talking among themselves.

'Aren't the dock gates the other way, Chief?' Khan enquired, pointing in the opposite direction towards the stern of their ship.

'You're right, Khan.' It dawned on them that these three women were not heading home after all.

John was the first to understand. 'You know what? We didn't give them any cash. They didn't ask, of course. But they can't go back without money,' he remarked wryly.

'So what?' Khan didn't get it at first.

'*So what*?' John repeated the question sardonically. 'Do you know what's going to happen if they don't make enough by morning? Their pimp's not going to be happy at all. He'll probably slash her other wrist!' The older seaman looked accusingly at Tony, who now realised what Lily had been trying to implore silently.

The three seamen watched guiltily without a word as Goldilocks and her two colleagues reached the Liberia-flagged cargo vessel berthed just ahead of theirs, and started trudging up that gangway.

4

The Hijack

'I wake up sweaty, I go to bed sweaty and I get out of the shower sweaty...*bwisit*![1]'

Ordinary Seaman (OS) Mark Carpio cursed under his breath and bemoaned his fate. Just nine days on board this huge, old oil tanker and he was already fed up. The air-conditioning just didn't work in the summer heat, the ship was trading in the warmest and the most dangerous area in the world, and he was being sent on deck for some unnecessary work, a sitting target for any pirate in a boat to take a potshot at him.

It was a hot afternoon in June 2009, and the threat of Somali piracy in and around the Gulf of Aden hung in the warm desert air. The Very Large Crude Carrier (VLCC) *Loboc River* cleared the Bab El Mandeb Strait at the southern end of the Red Sea and turned eastward into the pirate-infested waters of the Gulf of Aden. The coast of Somalia lay to her south. With a top speed of less than 13 knots and stretching to a length of more than 300 metres from weather-beaten bow to rusting stern, the grey behemoth had just entered the world's most dangerous shipping lane with a cargo worth USD 150 million, loaded just a few days ago at the Red Sea port of Yanbu in Saudi Arabia.

Two days earlier, the crew of twenty-six Filipinos of the *Loboc River* had set up the standard deterrents a merchant vessel crew uses to defend themselves against pirates. Around the deck's perimeter they had fitted coils of razor wire, rigged eight high-pressure water hoses aimed for blasting attackers off the hull, and propped up a scarecrow in overalls at the stern, to suggest the presence of a watch.

[1] *Bwisit:* Expletive (in Tagalog) expressing frustration.

Laughable when one is up against AK-47 assault rifles and rocket-propelled grenades that the pirates carry with them in speedboats, but this is a cold, hard fact even today that merchant seamen are left to fend for themselves against armed pirates. They are not allowed to carry weapons on board, nor given any military training in self-defence.

In the Steering Gear compartment of the ship, below deck and at the aft end, the crew had stocked the space—the 'citadel' as it is optimistically called—with food, water, portable radios and medical supplies, a refuge to hold out for several days in the event pirates did board the vessel. It had strong steel doors which could be bolted from inside to prevent attackers from entering from either deck or the Engine Room, but would not be able to withstand the blast of a grenade. Seamen are basically simple folk. They have faith in God and their superiors. In that order.

This crew too believed that an event such as a hijacking would not take place. Not to them anyway; they would be protected by those sworn to look after their well-being—their Captain, their ship-owner, their Company and God. The Powers That Be. Not necessarily in that order, though. They had heard from the Captain that their company, a Hong Kong-based one called Makati Fortune Investments Ltd, had arranged for a small security team of armed guards to rendezvous off the Yemeni port of Aden, to escort them through the most dangerous part of their journey—the Gulf of Aden—on their journey to the Far East. That gave them a feeling of comfort. The Head Office orders were neither to wait to be a part of a naval convoy nor to join a group transit of vessels, the two options most ship-owners opt for, but to sail alone at full speed, following the Internationally Recommended

Transit Corridor (IRTC) in the Gulf of Aden with armed escorts on board. Capt. Enrico Castro had delivered this bit of news to them during a briefing, shortly after sailing from Yanbu.

Twilight followed sunset, giving way to a clear evening sky when Mark at dinner felt the throb of engines subside. The ship must be off Aden, he guessed correctly. The *Loboc River* had stopped to await the security team which would come out of the harbour in a speedboat to meet the ship. They were about 7-8 nautical miles off the Yemeni coast. The ship drifted and waited. It was calm and silent, apart from the hum of generators and the sloshing of waves breaking against the rusty hull.

Assigned to be lookout on the bridge on that evening watch from 8 pm to midnight, Mark dutifully paced the bridge wings on both port and starboard flanks of the ship to spot any suspicious craft visually, while also going into the wheelhouse occasionally to look for any targets on the radar. Soon, expectedly he saw a blip on both radars, a target approaching fast. Through a pair of binoculars, he could discern in the moonlight a motorboat coming towards them. As it came close, Mark switched on the searchlight located on the bridge wing and directed the beam on the boat. He could make out seven people—six of them in desert-style camouflage, holding what looked like rifles. His superior on the watch, Third Officer Glen Padilla, called Capt. Castro in his cabin to brief him, and sent Mark down on deck to receive the security team. The boat was by then alongside.

'Good evening. Please identify yourself,' Mark yelled down to the boat, trying to sound friendly.

One of the men produced a megaphone. 'We are the security team. We need to board.'

Something wasn't right, Mark suspected. They were expecting a team of three, not six. These were too many men, and one wasn't even wearing shoes. Letting armed strangers onto the ship went against every antipiracy protocol.

'Okay, just a moment,' Mark called out to them and radioed up for instructions.

Capt. Enrico Castro's voice replied tersely, 'Lower the ladder.'

Six men climbed up. They had light brown skin and wore blue hospital masks. Their rifles looked like AK-47s, and they carried black pistols in holsters on their hips.

'Your IDs, please,' Mark requested them, as he was supposed to do. To his surprise they collared him, seized his radio, and demanded to be taken to the Captain.

The Captain was on the bridge with the Third Officer when Mark appeared at the door, trailed by one of the armed visitors. 'Gather all of the crew in the Recreation Room!' the gunman demanded, without any greeting. He had a guttural accent which Mark couldn't quite place.

Mark, his heart palpitating now that he was certain something was seriously wrong, went from cabin to cabin, accompanied by two gunmen, rousing sleepy crewmates. Soon all twenty-six crew members, barring the Captain who was asked to remain on the bridge accompanied by a gunman, were hustled into the Crew Recreation Room. This was a fairly large Common Room with seating; it had a large TV set and a dart board on the wall. The crew, now fully aware that they had lost control of their ship, sat down on the chairs, sofas and the carpet, trembling with trepidation. The five gunmen split up. Muttering instructions in what sounded like Arabic, one went back to the bridge, two marched Chief Engineer Adolfo Verchez to the Engine Room, and two stood sentry outside.

The crew waited and waited, stoically resigned to the fate that was to befall them. It would have been futile to revolt. Twenty-four sailors just sat there, silent, wondering what was going to happen to their Captain and Chief Engineer. And, later to themselves.

Suddenly there was a clatter of gunshots. They feared the worst, but dared not open the door. Mark's stomach churned, wondering if they would be fired upon next. But the door remained shut. After some time, the ship's engine roared to life. Its steady throb told them that they were moving. But no one knew where. They looked out of the porthole, but it was too dark to see. They waited.

At around 11 pm, there was a sudden jolt and an explosion sounded within the tanker, knocking out the electricity and setting off the alarms. The engine stopped. Fearful of their guards, the crew still waited in place, trying not to panic. But when smoke began to fill the room, a few crept out. The sentries outside the door were nowhere to be seen.

The fire seemed to come from below, probably the Engine Room, and was rising. The crew rushed up the stairs, away from the source of fire, guided by dim emergency lights that were designed to glow when there was a power outage. Mark and several others rushed into the bridge to find Capt. Castro alone in the pilot chair, bound by nylon rope. They untied him free. As smoke poured out of the tanker's funnel, the Second Officer made a distress call on the VHF radiotelephone and sounded the distress signal.

'Mayday, mayday, mayday! This is the *Loboc River, Loboc River, Loboc River*! I am on fire!' He shouted into the VHF handset.

'*Loboc River,* this is the *USS Houston*. I hear you.' The American accent was unmistakable.

The *USS Houston,* a guided-missile cruiser on pirate patrol nearby, assured the distressed crew they were on their way. Amid the collective sigh of relief, the Captain gave the order to abandon ship. He also informed the US warship of his intentions.

Nobody needed to be told twice. The smoke was rising in the accommodation block, and wisps trickling into the wheelhouse through the closed door were making the crew sweat and cough. Everyone, including the Captain, went down to the main deck from the outside companionways, to an area just forward of the accommodation. On the deck, a head count was taken. Twenty-five men—all but Chief Engineer Verchez—were accounted for. There was no gunman to be seen. They recalled that Verchez had been taken down to the Engine Room to probably start the engine, but a raging fire now seemed to be coming from that space.

The tall metal walls of the accommodation structure were radiating heat as the fire spread inside the crew's living quarters. They could hear loud, ominous cracks from metal buckling in the heat. Soon the two million barrels of crude oil in the cargo tanks under their feet would reach ignition point and explode. Panic set in. There was neither time nor inclination to organise a search party; the smoke coming out from the accommodation was now thick and dark.

The crew rushed to the port side lifeboat. It was swung out to deck level and the crew got in hurriedly. The Second Officer lowered it to water level from inside the boat by pulling on the remote control wire for launching. When the boat hit the water's surface, he started the lifeboat engine and released the hooks by operating the self-release mechanism to cut loose from the ship. As they moved away, the thrum of rotors from above told them to their relief that an airborne helicopter was near. It was an US Navy Seahawk helicopter, launched by the approaching *Houston*, which had easily caught the bright orange lifeboat in its searchlight. A cheer went up among the crew inside that stuffy, enclosed space.

From the air, the American helicopter pilot saw fireballs rising from the stricken tanker and felt the percussive boom of explosions within. The American crew trained infrared cameras on the hull seeking signs whether the oil—eight times the volume of the *Exxon Valdez* spill in 1989, an incident which had rocked the maritime world—would pour into the water. The lifeboat made its way to the side of the naval ship, a rope ladder was thrown down, and one by one all twenty-five Filipinos climbed up to be safely aboard the *Houston*.

The helicopter continued to monitor the burning tanker. Suddenly, at around 1 am, the helicopter crew saw movement on deck, a man frantically waving a flashlight. Chief Engineer Verchez was alive! It had to be him. The flames were too intense for an aerial rescue. The pilot saw him leap into the sea. The chopper hovered above the casualty, lowered a rescue line with a harness and hoisted him up by winch to safety.

Aboard the naval cruiser, the ship's crew, particularly the senior officers of the burning tanker were questioned intensively by the Americans. Capt. Castro's story was that after he was left alone on the bridge, the hijackers had ordered him to turn over all the ship's cash and sail for Somalia. They had dragged him to his own bedroom where the ship's safe was located and fired their weapons at the safe when he was fumbling for the keys. They had taken all the money in the safe—about USD 20,000—and brought him back to the bridge, roughed him up a bit, tied him up and left. He couldn't say what caused the explosion. When Verchez was asked to give his version of the events that took place, he said that after being forced at gunpoint to start the engine, he'd managed to disable the *Loboc River's* engines when his captors weren't looking, then escaped, hiding for so long among the mooring ropes in the Steering Flat that he had no idea that the rest of the crew had abandoned ship. OS Mark too gave his own account of receiving the visitors, being forced to take them to the bridge and gathering all the crew from their respective cabins to assemble in the Recreation Room.

The *USS Houston* searched for fleeing pirates, but the motorboat was long gone. Dawn came to soften the sky to a powdery blue and the clouds blushed ripe like mangoes. The outline of the smoking tanker turned clear. A tugboat, summoned by the US Navy, had already arrived from Aden and was pumping seawater on to the *Loboc River*, taming the fire and cooling the metal, until the dead tanker drifted serenely in the morning light, with just a column of fading smoke as a horrific reminder of the previous night.

Everyone at sea that night survived. But the chain of events had just begun.

Barely twelve hours had passed since the gunmen had taken over the ship. But already an international cast was activating. Salvage companies from the region's major ports were keen to scavenge millions from the wreckage. The US military investigators wanted to determine if Somali pirates had adopted brutal new tactics. Marine insurance experts from London wanted to discover what had really happened aboard a ship containing USD 150 million worth of liability. International news media homed in to show the world yet another manmade disaster.

Anytime a commercial vessel is lost, the incident is recorded at Lloyd's, a London-based institution that blends age-old ritual with modern finance. Lloyd's of London today is a society of marine insurers or underwriters, as they are commonly known in marine parlance. These marine insurance companies form syndicates, pool in their resources and insure hull, machinery and cargo of thousands of ships afloat. They get insurance of their own from even larger re-insurers, who are re-re-insured in turn. These layers constitute one of the world's most essential and least understood markets. Some fifty or more major vessels are lost each year, and the *Loboc River* was the largest of 2009. There was a lot of money at stake here, and the underwriters for this vessel were worried.

After a shipwreck, the insurers and the insured alike have an interest in preserving as much value as possible; so they turn to salvage. Salvors are entitled to a percentage of anything they save from destruction. In some of the murkier dealings that take place, it is rumoured that some ship-owners steer business to favoured salvage companies in return for a cut of the compensation that is claimed from insurance. So, there is a lot of scope for fraud.

The morning after, the tanker's owner, Makati Fortune, contacted a Dubai-based company named Neptune Salvage International, which got two of its boats in Aden to the scene by 10 am, to keep an eye on the ship and make arrangements to tow it to safety. One of the tugs took on all the shipwrecked crew from the naval warship and brought them ashore to Aden.

Two days later, Makati's owner, a Hong Kong Chinese named George Chan, flew to Aden. He met the *Loboc River's* crew staying at a hotel and gave each sailor USD 200 for new clothes. On a rather larger scale, he also prepared to submit a claim for his ruined supertanker.

But before the insurers would pay, they would want a better understanding of the hijacking. And for that, they turned to John Williams.

Every port, no matter how remote, has a small corps of marine surveyors, without whom Lloyd's and global shipping would cease to function. Surveyors are investigators hired to establish the facts of incidents from routine collisions to deadly storms; their assessments often make the difference between payment and denial of a claim. Many are former sea captains, who develop the skills of private investigators and execute them in perilous situations. John Williams was such a man, and the top marine surveyor in Aden.

When Williams got the *Loboc* assignment, Neptune's head salvor, a gnarled Greek diving expert, refused to give him access to the wreck for almost a week—an unusual and unexplained delay. This aroused Williams' suspicion, and he finally chartered a fishing trawler to get to the tanker, where the Greek insisted on accompanying him on his inspection.

The ship, groaning in heavy seas, had a deceptive appearance—the exterior was largely intact, while the mechanical and crew sections within were a total ruin. As Williams began exploring, his boots splashed through deep puddles of oily seawater left behind by three days' of firefighting. Inside the accommodation block, the beam from his flashlight swung left and right, illuminating blackened metal contorted by heat and crusted with soot. Every few steps, he paused to take photos. The engine room, where the fire had begun, was half-flooded, with ladders that descended into inky sludge. It was too dangerous to go deeper.

On his way back to Aden, Williams contemplated the strangeness of what he'd seen. Over the next several days, he discussed his suspicions over tea in his office with friends, paging through hundreds of photos on his laptop. He had a reputation as a careful, by-the-book surveyor, hesitant about inference or speculation.

The *Loboc* evidence didn't add up. And when he reviewed accounts given by the crew, he found them bizarre.

As he prepared his report, Williams shared his misgivings with all and sundry—some local colleagues, some from overseas.

'Can someone please explain to me why on earth would the pirates start a fire when they already had the ship and crew under their control?' Williams held forth to anyone who would listen, and there were many who did. 'They didn't need to do that! Pirates don't destroy ships they hijack—they hold the crew, cargo and ship for bloody ransom! So why would they start a fire? How did they cause an explosion to start the fire? They didn't use any rocket-propelled grenades, which is standard pirate tactic. Was it a hidden bomb?

'Why would they attack a ship at night in darkness, gentlemen? As a rule, they never do—they need the light of day to do so. It's also hard to believe an experienced captain would invite armed men onto his ship in the middle of the night, in the world's most dangerous waterway, if there was any question about their identity. The entire rendezvous strikes me as suspicious, gents. The Gulf of Aden is an area to accelerate through, not dawdle in!'

He talked, colleagues listened. And spread the word.

'And these chaps were light skinned and spoke Arabic—the crew was very sure about that. You know what Somalis look and talk like, right? They're pretty dark! These guys were neither Somali nor pirates. If you ask me, they were rogue elements of the Yemeni Coast Guard or Navy. And, why is the VDR of the ship—the black box—indicating the ship travelled west? Somalia is due bloody south!

'One more thing that puzzles me—how could the pirates have known that the ship was expecting a security team? That's how they introduced themselves, remember?'

He was met with silence and stares, some hard, some indifferent, and the occasional shrug of the shoulders to whomsoever he voiced his concerns. Nobody seemed to either support his theories or challenge them. Undeterred, by the last week of June, he sent off a detailed report to his Head Office in London, suggesting fraud, with a promise to explain more in a subsequent one. A world away at Lloyd's in London, tens of millions of dollars in insurance pay-outs hinged on Williams' findings.

The next day, at about 1 pm, Williams took his laptop, left his office, and climbed into his car. He normally made the short drive to his small house in a neighbouring district every day for lunch. That afternoon the street was empty. Williams had driven a short distance onto Aden's main street, when the bomb that had been carefully placed under his seat detonated. The blast was focused and powerful, loud enough to be heard blocks away. It killed Williams instantly, almost blowing his door off its hinges. As the car burned, belching smoke into the hazy sky, a crowd of locals in traditional white caps pushed toward the flames, shouting. Williams' body lay on the street next to the broken door, one arm extended, as if reaching for something.

The murder was shocking even in a chaotic city on the verge of revolution, accustomed to bombings. It remains unsolved till date.

By late July, what remained of the *Loboc River* was anchored in safe waters off the United Arab Emirates, towed there by Neptune's salvage tugs. Investigations however, continued. With the tanker finally secure, its decks bustled with small teams of inspectors taking measurements and photos, joined by fire and explosives experts and marine surveyors, hired by the insurers of both ship and cargo.

One of the explosives experts entered a space adjacent to the engine room, which had been drained and looked like the inside of a barbecue, and spotted an unmistakable bulge in a metal plate on the floor. It could only have been left by a bomb, he reported.

Accusations and allegations flew to and fro between ship-owner and Randall Underwriting Ltd, the insurance syndicate that had been formed by a group of ten companies of hull and machinery insurers facing huge claims. The salvage company Neptune Salvage International was asking for about USD 30 million as a reward for saving the oil cargo. George Chan's company Makati Fortune Investments Ltd wanted ultimately to recover about USD 100 million, covering the hull, machinery, and forgone profits, plus interest, from the syndicate Randall

Underwriting Ltd. Randall took an aggressive approach, denying Makati's claim for the ship, citing fraud. Makati sued in response.

To prepare for trial, the insurers sent investigators to Hong Kong and Singapore, to find out more about Makati's owner, George Chan. Some new facts came to light.

The investigators learned that one of Chan's ships had been in trouble off the coast of South Africa earlier. In May 2007, a 150,000-ton oil tanker called the *Agusan* had suffered an unexplained accident in perfectly good weather and fairly calm waters off Durban, splitting in half like a watermelon. The resulting claim, for about USD 35 million, was disputed by the ship's insurers and ended up in litigation. The parties had settled before trial.

The *Agusan's* Master at that time was Enrico Castro, and the Chief Engineer Adolfo Verchez. The salvage company that was first on the scene when the ship broke in two was Neptune International. Quite a series of coincidences.

George Chan had kept his name out of the *Agusan* litigation. He'd owned the tanker—as he did the *Loboc River*—through a web of anonymous offshore companies. Although trade publications indicate that Chan owned as many as eight large ships, he was for years virtually unknown to his insurers, even as his vessels sometimes came to tragic ends. Back in 1996, the *Ocean Lady*, an aging bulk carrier Chan owned was due to be scrapped. He sent it on one last journey, hauling ore from Brazil to China. It sank in a storm 2,000 miles west of Cape Town, one of the most remote places on earth, a thousand miles from nowhere, killing all twenty-four of its sailors. George Chan was charged with causing the deaths by negligence. But he was cleared for lack of evidence. The fact that there were no witnesses left alive to testify greatly helped his cause.

In 2011, after more than two years of preparation and compiling evidence, Randall Underwriting accused Chan of orchestrating the assault on the *Loboc River*. 'This was no attack by Somali pirates,' they said in documents filed in the High Court of London. 'Any such attack on the vessel was staged,' they continued, 'with the involvement and connivance of the Owner and members of the crew,' specifically naming Captain Castro and Chief Engineer Verchez as Chan's 'hit men'. The insurers claimed the fire was strategic—started by a bomb at a chosen location, and intended to scuttle the ship. The late John Williams' report, the only report that he had sent to his Head Office, proved invaluable.

Seeking to establish a motive, the insurers during the trial said that George Chan was deeply in debt, having borrowed USD 60 million or more to buy his ships, and that the *Loboc River* was losing money. Randall alleged that as his finances deteriorated, Chan plotted the destruction of the *Loboc River* to claim insurance money. Chan responded by accusing the insurers of 'unfairly and irresponsibly' endangering his reputation. He denied the 'unfounded and wrongful allegations', adding in a court statement, that he was 'a respectable businessman, welcomed and widely respected in the business circles of Hong Kong and Singapore'.

George Chan lost the case in the High Court of London and was not paid a cent of his claim. He did not appeal. However, the cargo insurers paid salvors Neptune their full claim for saving the cargo, which was later offloaded from the stricken vessel. It is not known if the wily ship-owner got his customary cut from his favourite salvage company.

The *Loboc River*'s final destination, after being declared a Total Constructive Loss, was Gadani Beach, a shipbreaking yard on Pakistan's Arabian Sea coast. The ship was hauled onto the sand, stripped of anything of value, and torn apart, piece by piece, by workers who make just a few dollars a day.

George Chan continues to be active in Hong Kong, but keeps a low profile, a shadow in the murky world of shipping.

Scuttling or damaging a ship for the insurance money is, in some respects, an ideal crime. There are generally no witnesses, no evidence, and no law enforcement. The odds of getting away with it are good. Even when an accident has the odour of foul play, Lloyd's insurers almost always pay something, to avoid the unpleasantness of customer conflict and to keep the premiums rolling in.

But if the *Loboc River* wasn't a genuine hijacking—if it was an inside job, with a cover-up that extended to murder—then it had no precedent in scale or theatricality.

It was one of the most spectacular frauds in shipping history.

Mark Carpio is still sailing in another tanker company, older and wiser. He has been successful in evading interviews by the media, investigators and shipping officials all these years, and now things have cooled down. He now uses his middle name Alvin in his identity documents and also when he introduces himself to others. He is not the carefree, confident young man he once was. Quiet threats in a hotel room in Aden in 2009 and later on at his home in Manila by his former superiors and their henchmen have put paid to that. Alvin keeps his mouth shut and lives in quiet anonymity. He does not know where Capt.

Castro and Chief Engineer Verchez are, or what they are up to nowadays. Nor does he care, as long as he never meets them again.

He has tried his best to put the past behind him. But it is doubtful if he will be able to forget those tumultuous days and nights many years ago of a mysterious assault, a near-death experience, an unsolved murder and a ship that went to her graveyard without giving up all her secrets.

5
The Visitor

'Sea speed, Chief,' I told the Chief Engineer, and put the intercom handset down to look out at the wide, open sea. I felt on top of the world, my mind awash with exhilaration, as the ship picked up speed. Soon, the shores of the Canary Islands would be a speck on the horizon as we set course for Brazil.

I stepped out of the wheelhouse onto the bridge wing to savour the fresh breeze. The rippled sea was peaceful, and its soft murmurs scarcely audible. A line of darker blue marked the curve of the southern horizon. The wake of the ship, flecked with foam, left a straight white track against the dark contrast of the water. It is always a relief to sail out of a port and feel the fresh sea breeze tug at one's hair and eyelashes.

It was late afternoon and still bright—that is how I spotted them. A pigeon and a sparrow, hopping about on the main deck below. Two birds of different feathers flocking together. Unusual, I thought. Not just because you don't see many birds other than seagulls out at sea. Here were two different species of birds sticking together, forgetting their cultural differences, overcoming their racial prejudices if any, united in their bewilderment about the strange surroundings and probably terrified of the circumstance that had befallen them.

A pigeon and a sparrow. Well, to be honest, it may not have been a sparrow. But it certainly looked like one. White and brown. Plump and tiny. Since there were no distinguished ornithologists on board to identify the species, I decided to call it a sparrow. As you've probably heard, on a ship the Captain's word is final.

I watched our avian guests for a while, hopping here and there. But as it grew dark, I went down to my office to send my routine emails and thought no more about them.

Nor did they come to mind the next morning. But just before noon, while I was taking a walk on deck with Abhay, the Chief Officer and my next-in-command, we spotted the pigeon's dead body lying on the deck by the side.

'Oh, no!' I couldn't help exclaiming. It is always unnerving to have a death at sea of any kind, and a bad omen. It had probably died of hunger or thirst, or from a whiff of gas that may have leaked from a cargo tank. After all, we were on a large crude oil tanker in ballast with huge empty cargo tanks containing toxic vapours that had remained after having discharged our previous oil cargo in Europe. Who knows how it perished? I looked out for the little, plump sparrow and was relieved to see it still hanging about on the main deck, drinking from the puddles of rain water that had accumulated from a shower that morning.

Abhay and I looked at each other. We could read each other's minds, it seemed, and he nodded. Yes, the sparrow would be looked after. And no, the sparrow would not be allowed to meet the same fate.

On the second day I went up to the bridge, the control room which is manned round the clock at sea and from where the ship is navigated, early in the morning to have a cup of tea. Twilight had yielded to sunrise and it promised to be a fine day. To my pleasant surprise, I noticed the sparrow flying across my field of vision. In my preoccupation with mundane matters, I had again forgotten about the little bird. So, it had summoned the courage and strength to fly up several deck levels from the main deck and reach the bridge deck! It perched itself on the railing just across the front bridge windows and stared at us through the glass with, I thought, a reproachful look.

'I've put a bowl of water on both sides, Sir, knowing that the little fellow must be thirsty,' Abhay remarked with a smile, walking up to me. He manned the watch in the early mornings and early evenings at sea. Sure enough, the sparrow went to the bowl on the port (left) side bridge wing deck and drank greedily from it.

'Where is it staying? Still on the main deck?' I enquired.

Abhay didn't know. Nobody did. Over the next few days of the voyage, we would see it occasionally, generally when we were least expecting to. Here, there and everywhere. Sparrow sightings on the bridge at daybreak and at dusk became the norm. Someone said that it was staying under the port side life raft, someone else said on the poop deck at the aft end of the ship. But later we realised that it had made its home in the rain shelter on main deck forward of the accommodation.

We started feeding it, determined to keep it alive. Call it the superstition of seamen, call it what you will. But somehow the fortune of that sparrow was linked to ours on that ship and on that voyage—all twenty-four of us. If that sparrow went down, so would we—or so we feared.

The cook kept a few crumbs of food outside his galley, anxious that our guest did not starve to death. Chief Officer Abhay started refilling the bowls on either bridge wing every morning religiously so that the sparrow wouldn't go thirsty. We had no idea what it was eating or how it was managing for food. Abhay started keeping Danish cookies, crushed to little bits, on the port bridge wing every morning. The sparrow would come on the dot, and to our joy start nibbling at the cookie crumbs. It would fly away if any of us approached it. So, we stayed away and watched it peck vigorously at the food, at dawn and at dusk.

It became our mission to keep the sparrow alive. Every one of us became its foster parents, Abhay Apte in particular. Sparrow sightings were reported religiously. Like 'Chief Mate, we saw your sparrow on Upper Deck an hour ago', and suchlike. Like it had become *his* sparrow!

The little one relocated its residence on the fourth or fifth day. It was reported that it was staying on the wooden pallets below the swimming pool deck aft of the accommodation. I guessed it had discovered the comfort of wood, a familiar material, and wanted to lovingly peck at and scratch it, or do whatever sparrows like to do with wood.

'Doesn't the little bugger eat anything else?' I remarked to Abhay one day, puzzled, while observing it pecking at the little morsels of biscuit one evening. Apparently, it was not touching the crumbs the cook was putting out for him outside the galley. 'Come on, the cooking isn't that bad!' I added in jest to no one in particular.

We tried to change its diet. On the fifth day, Abhay put out crushed Skyflakes in a bowl. Skyflakes, in case you didn't know, are bland thin biscuits, mildly salty—standard fare on most ships. The sparrow nibbled at the crumbs initially, but wouldn't touch them again. The Skyflakes remained untasted. The little fellow was nowhere to be seen that day.

We feared the worst.

But no—on the sixth day, a sparrow sighting was reported to our immense relief.

'Looks like it doesn't like the taste of Skyflakes, Captain,' the Chief Engineer declared with great wisdom at the daily meeting, after hearing of the Skyflakes remaining untasted. Yes, another concerned parent.

There we were—on a long voyage, totally isolated from the world with just the horizon to look at, dull uneventful days blending with duller days of sheer routine, just twenty-four men from different countries and different cultures to keep each other company. Our feathered friend became our focus of interest. Something to talk about, someone to look after—a new entrant to our family.

That evening we asked the Able Bodied Seaman (AB) on duty, to bring more Danish cookies from the galley. I crushed a couple and put them out in the open on the bridge wing. The sparrow was immediately on to the sweet cookie crumbs as soon as we had moved away. It had a real sweet tooth after all. 'That's the way the cookie crumbles, I guess,' I announced, resigning myself to our feathered friend's food habits. Nobody got the pun, unsurprisingly. Mastery of the English language is not a merchant seaman's strong suit.

'You have to hand it to this little fellow, Sir,' Abhay remarked to me on the bridge that evening. 'This little fellow is a fighter, a real fighter, trying to survive against all odds! I often wonder if I were in its place, would I survive?'

This was absolutely true. A ship on the ocean is a strange, harsh environment not just for a little sparrow, but for any living creature. For the first time in its life, it was encountering cold steel, deafening noise, constant vibration, strong winds and a throbbing engine. There was no green foliage, no fellow birds and no wild life.

I looked at him and said, 'How do you know it'll survive? There's nothing going for the poor bugger, except us.' He nodded in agreement, a little worried.

On the seventh day, Abhay transferred a potted plant from inside the wheelhouse to the open spaces on the bridge wing, hoping that the bird would feel better by recognising something familiar to the habitat it had grown up in. A special container of plastic was prepared by the Bosun, another concerned foster parent, with areas for cookies, water and Skyflakes in it. But no, the bird wasn't interested in fine dining. It preferred to pick at cookies directly from the deck or wooden rail on the bridge wing—doing what came naturally.

Abhay would get the crew to wash the bridge deck twice a day. He did not want the soot that would occasionally fly from the ship's funnel to scatter about on the bridge wings, fearing the bird might peck at it and die of poisoning. The sparrow had become the darling of the ship's crew. The Bosun and Pumpman would enquire about it every morning when they reported to the Chief Officer for the day's work. Everybody wanted it safe. Everybody wanted it happy.

After eight days, the sparrow would not fly away even when one of us approached it. Provided we approached it cautiously, of course. Gradually an easy familiarity had grown. It began to feel safer and more secure in our presence.

We were retarding the ship's clocks every few days as we crossed time zones on our way to Brazil. But the bird's body clock or the clock in its mind did not change. It began to present itself at 4 pm ship's time for dinner, when the ship's clock had read 6 pm a few days earlier. In its mind...or rather in its stomach...it was dinner time, never mind the bright sun still well above the horizon.

One late afternoon, I was slowly pacing the deck of the wheelhouse. The sparrow was perched outside on the railing just in front of the bridge deck windscreen watching me. As I walked inside the wheelhouse in one direction, it hopped on the railing in the same direction trying to keep up with me. When I turned around and walked leisurely the other way, it did so too. It was amusing and very endearing, and kept all of us on the bridge that day fascinated. I stuck my hand out and threw cookie crumbs into the open. It flew and pounced on the food.

Ten–eleven days passed…the sparrow was no longer fleeing from us. In fact, I saw it once standing on the door frame of the half-open sliding door of the wheelhouse, twittering…maybe asking for permission to enter? It flew away after some time but was back ten minutes later and hopped right in. I guessed it felt claustrophobic after some time inside, and tried to fly away. But it kept hitting the nearest glass window, bewildered why it could not reach the open spaces it could see ahead and why it was getting hurt. I quickly opened the sliding door on the other side of the wheelhouse. It felt the breeze rush in and flew away through that door.

The next day the sparrow came in without much hesitation. It hopped about, perched itself on the table lamp of the chart table as if it were a tree branch. Quite comfortable in its new surroundings. It fluttered here and there—the engine control panel, the coffee machine, the gyro compass repeater—before flying out through the other door. This time it already knew the way out. Trust had developed; it knew that we meant no harm because we had also shown it the escape route.

'Check out this photo shoot, Sir,' Abhay told me the next morning. Sure enough, he had taken several photographs of his new best friend with his camera. From the pictures, it appeared that the sparrow had actually enjoyed the attention and the whole photo session. Not only had it not fled, it had actually preened and posed for a few of them, looked at the camera directly for some shots and had cocked its head at an angle for some others. Not camera shy at all. I still have a photograph of the little fellow.

We were a day away from the Brazil coast when the seagulls came in flocks. Raucous squawking, flapping their wide wings, a flurry of white feathers everywhere, flying about all over the ship, coating the deck and the side railings with their droppings. The sparrow again went AWOL. I asked around. Nobody on board had seen it. We were worried whether it had been attacked by one of these predators, killed, carried out into the ocean and dropped there. Where was it? I was concerned…we all were.

But there was good news the next day. The bird had been spotted by a seaman hiding under the wooden pallets under the swimming pool deck. It had sensed danger and had taken evasive action, adopting discretion as the better part of valour.

On the fourteenth day of the voyage, the ship arrived at Angra Dos Reis, Brazil. The voyage had ended. We were asked to drop anchor to wait for a berth. A swarm of insects—flies, moths and whatnot—reached the ship at the anchorage to welcome her to Brazil and settle on board as unwelcome guests. The air was abuzz with their presence. But where was the sparrow?

The sparrow, I was told, was having a wonderful time gobbling up these new arrivals. During those five days at anchor, every day was Feast Day for our little friend, as per the daily reports from its well-wishers. It did not come to the bridge even once for cookies or to say hello. It had enough to eat on the poop deck aft, pouncing on unsuspecting insects and devouring them. It did not need us now, it seemed.

On the evening before we sailed from Brazil, I saw the sparrow again. It again sat on the railing outside the front windows of the bridge, staring at me, while I was taking a walk in the wheelhouse. It was difficult to discern its expression in the fading light of dusk. Perhaps it wanted to say goodbye and thank me for my hospitality, before moving on? It had already sensed somehow that a familiar habitat of land and forest was near, and had decided to go there.

That was the last I saw of that little bird as it flew away. I would like to believe that it managed to get a Brazilian Permanent Resident visa, travelled into the forests of Brazil, found new friends, started a family perhaps and lived there happily ever after.

Wasn't it Darwin who said that it is not the strongest of the species that survive, or the most intelligent, but the ones most responsive to change? I'm not sure who said it, but believe me, it is true. I saw it with my own eyes. My little feathered friend, wherever you may be, I salute your survival skills. I hope you've got your life back, and are regaling your friends with your sea stories as I write this.

6

Miss Me?

Madhu (in Jaipur)

Sunday 12th October 2014

Shyam should have come home by now. Ever since he went back to the ship in April, he has been so uncommunicative. Earlier he used to call so often. His tour of duty must be over. More than six months have passed… why doesn't he call? I asked *Bhaiyya* to look up the Internet to find out where his ship is. I believe you can trace any ship in the world on the Internet. But when *Bhaiyya* asked me the name of the ship, I realised I did not know. Shyam never told me the name, and I never asked!

I have his Mumbai office number. I'll ask Papa to call them tomorrow.

Once I know when he is coming, I am going to take a couple of trips to the beauty parlour and go all glamorous. I want to see the look in his eyes when he sees the new me! Madhu Gupta…sizzling hot! He always criticises me for not being city bred, not being fluent in English, not being too educated. So what if he went to a good English medium school and knows English songs? He says I should have done my graduation in English or Psychology or History, not Home Science. His talk does hurt me, but I know he is a good man. He just wants the best for me, I am sure.

Shyam (on the ship)

Saturday 11th October 2014

I think it is going to work out. After all, I've been planning this for a long time now. Vanish. No traces. Disappear among the teeming millions in this country. Start a new life with Joyce in Shillong. Or Imphal, maybe?

I'm cash rich now. Collected my entire salary of six months in cash; did not send any remittance to my bank. All my papers are with me—there are no other documents I need. I can get a new identity once I settle down in the north-east. Joyce said that she knew somebody who knew somebody who had managed to get a false passport in Kohima. I'm good to go, man!

The office has sent details of my relief to the Captain. Shouldn't be long now. I have asked as usual to be repatriated to Mumbai, my 'home port'. From there I'm supposed to take the train home. Except that I won't be on that train.

Madhu, will you miss me?

Madhu (in Jaipur)

Friday 17th October 2014

Something is not right. Papa called to tell me that he had contacted the Mumbai office. They told him that Shyam had already signed off the ship on the 14th somewhere in France—I don't remember the name of the port he mentioned—and had taken the flight to Mumbai on the same day. As per the ticket he should have arrived at Mumbai on 15th morning. But when Papa told them that he had not arrived home yet, the *officewalas* said that their responsibility ended when the seaman arrived at his 'home port'. After that any outstation seaman was supposed to make his own arrangements to travel home. That is a fact, I know. It is written in the contract Shyam signs every time with his employers. He always flies back to Mumbai and then takes the train home to Jaipur. He may not have got a train ticket. But he can fly, no? So where is he?

Madhu (in Jaipur)

Monday 20th October 2014

I went to the local police station this morning. Didn't like that Sub-Inspector Ajay Kumar—the way he was eyeing me. When I told him that my husband was missing, he smirked and remarked that it was not illegal for a person to go missing. But I insisted on filing a Missing Person's Report. Reluctantly, he took out two sheets of foolscap paper from a drawer full of rubbish and started writing slowly. He was full of questions—so tiresome!

'Name, Madam?'

'Height? Weight? Hair colour? Eye colour? Build? Birthmarks? Tattoos?' and so on.

Then 'Clothing? Shoes?' How would I know what he was wearing when he reached Mumbai?

'Friends? Girlfriends?' He looked up from his writing mockingly when he asked me these questions. Insolent man! I have a good mind to report him to his superiors.

'Medical condition? Allergies?' None that I knew of.

'So what makes you think he is missing?'

He went on and on. But at least he seemed to be doing his job.

I answered patiently all the questions he asked, giving that cop as much information as I could. I gave him two fairly recent photographs of Shyam that I had. He gave me a copy of the handwritten report. It had a stamp, an FIR number and the date on it.

Ajay Kumar told me that he would investigate and call me as soon as he had some information. I wish he had looked at my face instead of my breasts when he said that. All men are the same…so annoying!

As I was heading home, it dawned on me that I did not really know my husband that well. I met him for the first time when our parents arranged the meeting. I liked him immediately, of course, but now I wonder if he liked me as much. Was there someone in his life before we had this typical arranged marriage? He was always evasive when I asked him this. His professional life too is a shadow world, a world apart which he never shares with me. He never once asked me to join him on the ship during the three years that we have been married. I had hinted to him a few times that I wanted to go, but he had always demurred, giving excuses like the cabins were too small or I'd get seasick or something like that.

I called up Papa when I reached home. He told me not to worry, and wait. But he didn't sound so confident himself. Shyam, where are you?

Shyam (in Gurgaon)

Saturday 9th March 2013

I think I am in love. Yesterday I met the girl of my dreams. Joyce.

I had come to Gurgaon to attend a friend's wedding, leaving Madhu at home. Thank God I did that. Otherwise I'd never have met this babe.

Joyce Khongmen. Pretty as a picture, smooth hairless skin, lovely straight dark hair. Almond-shaped eyes, high cheekbones. Exquisite! Speaks English so well, and knows all the English songs. Seems to like me too. We were at a Cyber City pub when a common friend introduced us. She is working with Convergys BPO looking after customers of Orange, the multinational telecom company. Lived in Shillong before she came here. I'll have to look up Google Maps to find out where that is. Don't know much about the north-east. Who the fuck does?

'Chinky', those louts at her BPO call her. She laughs it off, but I know it hurts her. Those damned North Indian lechers, filled to the brim with testosterone and lust. Laughing at her convent-educated English and proper manners. I find her oriental looks captivating. She is so sweet and kind.

I told her I was a Merchant Navy officer. She seemed impressed. I didn't tell her I was married, though. Just a technicality, isn't it?

Shyam (in Gurgaon)

Saturday 11th May 2013

I can't believe it... I slept with Joyce last night! She is as lovely as I'd imagined her to be. Golden brown skin like satin, shy smile, dark, long hair spread like a storm upon the pillow. We have become pretty close to each other over the past couple of months. I talked her into coming to bed with me and, to my surprise, she agreed. We booked a room at the Jukaso Inn in Sector 14. It was a heavenly night.

Coming to Gurgaon regularly from Jaipur is no problem. All I have to tell that cow Madhu is that my employer is making me do all these essential refresher courses, without which I will not get a job at sea. The cow sulks for a while and then gets over it. It's partly true—I *am* attending courses by day. But during the nights in Gurgaon I intend to attend lovemaking courses lying in Joyce's arms. We are meeting in secret now; telling none of our common friends.

I wish I didn't have to go back home. Or back to sea. Can't bear to leave this angel.

Madhu (in Jaipur)

Friday 31st May 2013

Shyam is all packed and ready to go back to the ship. He seems preoccupied all the time nowadays. Hardly ever smiles or talks to me. He's always on that mobile phone of his sending or receiving text messages. I know he has a lot of friends in Gurgaon, he told me so. But surely he should spend time with me also? I don't like it when he goes away so frequently to Gurgaon or wherever on work.

When I suggested to him the other day that maybe we should start a family of our own, he looked aghast. He said he needed time, that it was too early. Too early? We've been married for two years now. Mummy is asking me all the time when we intend to have a child.

Shyam (on the ship)

Tuesday 22nd October 2013

Yes, I have decided. Shyam Gupta will just disappear from the face of the earth. There is nothing to bring him home to Jaipur. He'll start a new life with Joyce somewhere, where nobody can find him.

But I have to really plan this out, don't want to screw it up. It may take six months, maybe a year. When I get back home this time, I'll have to do it step by step. In a year from now, all loose ends must be tied up. If Madhu or that annoying brother of hers goes to the cops, they may get on my trail.

I must get rid of the plastic. No debit or credit cards, too easily traceable. Just cash henceforth.

I must deactivate my Facebook, LinkedIn, Google+ and Twitter profiles in due course. Just disappear from the virtual world. Nobody should be able to contact me or my online friends for information. In any case, nobody knows that Joyce and I are a couple. We've been careful about that.

When I get home, I must quietly destroy as many photographs of mine as I can find. The less the cops see of me, the better. But Madhu has a private stash of pictures lying somewhere. Must find that too. Don't want family and friends running around town with my photos asking too many questions.

Freedom, freedom...here I come!

Shyam (in Jaipur)

Tuesday 21st January 2014

I have started moving my assets to cash. Madhu was delighted when I opened a fixed deposit of Rs 20 lakhs for her. If she only knew that this would be the last bit of money she's ever going to get from me. It should be enough to tide her over. She'll be okay—her dad is quite well off. The rest of the cash I will move in regular amounts to safety deposit boxes—one in Gurgaon, one in Mumbai. Need to make regular trips to both places on some pretext or other.

Just wondering...how far will they go to find me? How much will her dad be willing to spend?

I will miss a lot of things, I know. My car, Mom, the dog, my collection of CDs, DVDs, my books...but they just have to remain where they are. Won't take anything that will remind me of my home and the past that I am leaving behind. No excess baggage, literally and metaphorically. I must travel light, and I must be strong!

Just now cut up my plastic debit and credit cards into little pieces and threw them into the garbage bin. There! Cash it is from now on.

I told Joyce of the plan. She is thrilled! I'm so relieved to see the expression of joy on her lovely face. She wasn't happy earlier when I told her I was married, but I managed to convince her that it had been a mistake, and that it was she who I wanted to spend the rest of my life with.

The plan still needs a lot of work though. We must go far away from here, the two of us. I told her to tell no one, not a soul.

'Come to Shillong, Shyam!' Joyce said excitedly, 'You'll love it! There are pine forests, lakes, waterfalls! There are rolling, green hills all around the town!'

Sounds good to me. I'll go anywhere you want me to, babe. Nobody will think of looking for us there. Nobody looks for people in the north-eastern part of India anyway.

Madhu (in Jaipur)

Monday 3rd November 2014

No sign of Shyam. When I called up that Sub-Inspector Ajay Kumar, he said that there were no leads.

'Maybe he does not want to be found, Madam,' he remarked. I could hear the smirk in his voice. What did he mean by that?

Bhaiyya told me that he could not find any trace of Shyam on any of the social networking sites. I called up his local friends. They all were surprised to hear he is missing. No, they did not know any friends of his in Gurgaon.

I again called up that Sub-Inspector to ask him to trace some leads in Gurgaon. Shyam used to go there often on work. Maybe somebody has some information there.

I was wondering if I should hire a private investigator. But they are quite expensive, I hear. I don't want to be taken for a ride by them, charging me (Papa actually) on a daily basis and after two weeks saying they can't find him.

My fears seem to be coming true. The way Shyam has wiped his traces, it appears that he doesn't want to be found. I think the policeman has a point.

Shyam (on the ship)

Tuesday 30th September 2014

I called up Joyce today from the ship. My heart went aflutter on hearing her voice—like the tinkling of silver bells. I gave her the plan which she was to execute. She had already tendered her resignation a month ago, and was just waiting in Gurgaon for my instructions. I told her to open my safety deposit box with the key I had given her and withdraw all the cash in it. She was to travel to Shillong by train, not air, and rent an apartment. She was to divulge her plans to nobody. She was to email the address to me at the new ID I have opened under an assumed name. I would be getting off the ship in two weeks' time, make my way by bus or train and join her. We would start a new life together.

Can't wait!

Joyce (in Gurgaon)

Tuesday 30th September 2014

Shyam called today. It is really happening! I am so excited and yet so scared. I haven't told Mom that I've quit my job—she will be so upset. How can I tell her that I am running away with a married man and coming back home, but can't meet her? Crazy! But I can't help it. I love this man, and I want to spend the rest of my life with him. Shyam has assured me repeatedly that everything will work out fine, and I believe him. He'll take care of everything, I know. We'll be happy together.

Shyam (in Mumbai)

Wednesday 15th October 2014

Arrived at Mumbai airport at the crack of dawn. Bought a ticket under my own name for Chennai. That is money well spent, I think, to throw them off the track. That is one flight I am not going to take. Withdrew all my cash from the safety deposit box where I had hidden my earnings after encashing my assets. Then I took a suburban train to Thane. Changed my dollars for a huge amount of rupees at a travel agent outside the railway station. Now I'm really cash rich—must be careful and remain inconspicuous.

Bought a train ticket to Kamakhya at the Thane station. Although a long train journey ahead, it is safer that way. I can travel incognito. From Kamakhya to Gauhati airport by cab, then two hours by bus to Shillong. I'll have Joyce in my arms by Friday afternoon. Yes!

I will need to change my appearance a bit. Colour my hair, grow a beard. It's good I was wearing that baseball cap at the airport. They have these CCTV cameras everywhere nowadays. Damn!

Madhu (in Jaipur)

Friday 7th November 2014

The Sub-Inspector called. Asked me to come to the station. Trying not to look at my breasts, he told me that Shyam was last spotted at Mumbai airport having arrived on the flight from Dubai on the 15th morning. He was wearing a cap to cover his features, so the police could not be 100 percent sure. Shyam then bought a ticket to fly to Chennai, but did not take the flight. He then left the airport and has not been traced since.

'It looks as if he is trying to cover his tracks, Madam,' Ajay Kumar said with gravity. 'I don't think he wants to come back.' He shrugged his shoulders and added, 'It is not illegal to want to go missing, you know.' He keeps saying this.

Not illegal? What about my life that he has ruined? Is that legal?

Now I realise how Shyam has been fooling me for more than a year. I feel lost in his lies. What has replaced my anxiety is now a sense of betrayal. What a fool I've been!

Madhu (in Jaipur)

Wednesday 10th December 2014

No further news of him. He really planned this carefully. I know he is alive and well somewhere. Just doesn't want to be with me. Papa told me that he will never let Shyam return to me. He and *Bhaiyya* are talking to lawyers trying to get the marriage annulled. Well, goodbye and good riddance, Mr Shyam Gupta. It looks like you won't be welcomed back.

Shyam (in Shillong)

Tuesday 2nd June 2015

Hmmm…it's been six–seven months here… it's been, well, okay… I mean the greenery, the quiet, the hill station life. But there are some things I hadn't foreseen. There is also dirt, litter, traffic, population and pollution! Everything is so expensive here in Shillong—the rent, electricity, groceries! I don't know how long my money will last. Not easy to get a job either if one is an outsider. It appears that jobs are available only if you're a Khasi or a Garo. So it doesn't look like I'll get work if I decide to look for a job. These *Chinks* seem openly hostile to me. The way they look at me suspiciously, and switch over to the local lingo the minute I approach them. But Joyce assures me that this is not so, it is the way they are. What the fuck does that mean?

The world looks almost fake sometimes to my jaundiced eye. Like the rolling hills, forests and sky in the distance are backdrops for a set. A green screen.

I miss the night life of Gurgaon. Heck! I'm beginning to miss Jaipur too—never thought I'd live to see that day! How long can one live in a hill station where you feel you don't belong?

I wonder what Madhu is doing. I wonder if she thinks of me at all. Do you miss me, Madhu?

Joyce (in Shillong)

Monday 15th June 2015

Shit… It is not as idyllic as I had hoped it would be. The first month was nice and like a romantic fairy tale.

But now? How long can we live like fugitives? That too in Shillong, where I did my schooling and lived for so many years? Shyam is so conspicuous. Too large, too hairy with that beard to blend with the crowd. He doesn't even try to mix with the locals. And the locals don't like him, though I keep assuring him that he's just imagining things. I can't make friends with anyone, because he fears I may give us away by some idle remark. He doesn't want me to take up a job here for the same reason. I didn't realise he was so domineering. So no friends, no job, nothing to do!

This vanishing act has taken its toll on us—I mean, like physically, mentally and emotionally. We are snapping at each other all the time now. I miss my mother and sisters. I miss my home.

I think I need to vanish too. Just disappear. No traces. Can't take it anymore. I'll go back to my village. It's not far from here. Back to my own family. He's getting a bit tiresome, and I can't live like this, no way. He will never let me go, I know. So I'll just have to slip away one dark night.

Shyam, will you miss me?

7

Reach for the Stars

They met at a café in the pavilion of Dowlat Park, in the port of Bandar Abbas, Iran. The café overlooked the grey-brown waters of the Strait of Hormuz, the entry point to the Arabian Gulf. Ships passed to and fro in the hazy distance below their horizon. A warm breeze blew in from seaward. Three grim men with hard, dark eyes looked him up and down as he approached. One by one they introduced themselves, shaking his hand as he sat down beside them at the table.

'Devinder,' said the Punjabi from India.

'Khalid,' the Pakistani introduced himself.

'Mustafa,' said the Iranian. This one seemed to be the leader among the group. He had a quiet air of authority which the other two lacked.

'Captain Rajan Tiwari,' he introduced himself. The others stared at him stonily, sizing him up.

Mustafa cleared his throat and began, 'Captain, you have already been briefed earlier by phone, but it is our duty to make sure that the orders are clear.' He spoke in good Hindi, with a Farsi accent. 'Ahmadi Sahib does not like mistakes.'

Tiwari gave a nod of his head in acknowledgement. He had never met Hasan Ahmadi, the Dubai-based Iranian who owned the ship Tiwari had been given command of, nor was he particularly keen to. Ahmadi's reputation preceded him.

'Before sailing from here, you will have to paint a different name on the bow and stern,' the Iranian continued, his dark eyes boring hard into Tiwari's to make sure he was listening. He used the words *'aage peechhey'* instead of the nautical terms *bow* and *stern*. 'The *Princess* will become *M.V.Julie*. Is that clear?'

Tiwari nodded, but enquired, 'What about the ship's certificates, her registry? The name should be changed on those too. Suppose port officials somewhere board to inspect the vessel?'

'Don't worry about that,' Khalid brushed aside the queries. 'New certificates will be delivered to you in two days' time. Including a Panama registry. After that, you must destroy the existing ones.'

Mustafa the Iranian continued, 'As we speak, you're aware that my gang of dock labour—welders and machinists and fitters—is creating cavities in your ship's ballast tanks, fresh water tanks and pipes to hide the consignment? Your cargo holds will remain empty. If any port authority asks you for your cargo manifest, you have nil cargo on board, okay?'

Tiwari nodded again.

'Still two days of work is to be completed before you sail, Captain,' Devinder spoke this time. 'After that, please familiarise yourself with the spaces that have been created. Our foreman will show you. All these spaces are to be utilised. You will pick up 1,526 packets—1,200 of pure white, the remainder will be *chitta*[1] from Gwadar—the *chitta* packets are marked differently—and head for Alexandria in Egypt, where they will be offloaded by our people there. Fifteen hundred kilos in total.'

'Exactly 1,526 packets have to reach Egypt, Captain. Not a single packet less.' Mustafa interjected. The hint in his steady gaze was ominous.

---

[1] *Chitta:* A synthetic drug mix of heroin and other substances, mainly manufactured in Punjab.

Tiwari could not help but feel uneasy.

After a little more discussion, the Iranian indicated by a wave of his hand that the meeting was over. 'You may go back to your ship now, Captain. You will hear from us again. Before you sail, we will give you the rendezvous position off Gwadar port where boats will come out to you with the consignment.'

Tiwari stood up, nodded to them and walked away. He could feel their eyes boring into his back.

Two days later, the ship *M.V.Julie* was ready to sail. The dock workers had done their job, and so had the ship's crew. The ship's new name was painted on the hull at the appropriate locations and she had new statutory certificates. Fake ones, of course. The makeover was complete.

Rajan Tiwari stood on the bridge wing that hot afternoon smarting with rage and indignation, as the ship left the port of Bandar Abbas behind. How dare these drug peddlers treat him like their paid servant? He was a Master Mariner qualified to command a merchant ship. Notwithstanding the small size of this one, he was still a merchant navy captain, not a lowlife criminal like those three. And what had he been promised for delivering this consignment to the buyer? A bonus of USD 10,000. And another ten to share among the crew. Ten lousy thousand for narcotics worth about thirty to forty million dollars? He was being treated like an interstate lorry driver, just to ferry goods from one place to another, and being paid the cab fare. No, he did not like it one bit.

Rajan Tiwari had always nurtured big dreams. Of humble origins, his father, a lowly paid clerk in the Bihar government, had struggled to make ends meet and put his two sons through school. Rajan was bitter, and nursed a grudge, about never having enough all his life, going hungry at times, and always having to struggle more than his peers at everything. But struggle he did. And hard work and determination paid off. A sea career was just the ticket for him to set his course on making his dreams come true. He cleared the entrance exams, came out to sea, took his career seriously, passed his promotional exams in good time and worked his way up the ladder. Now, at a relatively young age of twenty-nine, he was a Captain. So far, so good. But it wasn't enough.

He wanted to get rich, and rich quickly. He pursued wealth with breathless haste, almost hurrying past it—looking for the one big opportunity that would make him rich for life. A big house in a big city, a second vacation home in Goa, fancy cars, a good life for his wife and his parents, the best school in town for the kids he would one day have... He wanted all of these and more, and wasn't willing to wait too long. It was his firm belief that if you reach for the stars, you'll get there sooner or later. The sooner the better, of course.

On that afternoon, while standing on the bridge as he set course to seaward, he believed he had at last got that one big opportunity. A plan slowly began to take shape in his mind. But first the consignment had to be received on board before he could carry out the next part of his plan. And the next.

Thirty-six hours later, the lights of the port of Gwadar on the coast of Pakistan brought a yellow glow to the horizon when Tiwari stopped his ship twenty miles south from shore to start drifting at the rendezvous position. He waited. It was almost midnight. Half an hour later, the moonlight shone on the water like pale silver to illuminate the white wake of three motor boats that approached his vessel.

The crew got to work. The boats were made fast alongside. The consignments were picked in slings using the ship's crane, and landed on deck. Fifteen hundred kilos of pure white heroin and *chitta* were loaded. The boats left as quietly as they had come. The crew efficiently started hiding the plastic packets in places created on the ship for this purpose, where no one could detect their presence at first glance, though the cargo holds remained empty. While they were busy doing so, Tiwari made a few calls on the ship's satellite phone. The ship continued to drift in the moonlit night, the current taking her slowly seaward.

After the consignment was hidden from sight in all the secret places, he felt it was time for a talk with the crew. Blood racing through his veins, his hands shook with excitement. The phone calls made earlier had been fruitful, and now for the next part of the plan. He had to convince the crew to get on board with the plan. He wouldn't be able to carry this out without their cooperation.

He called them up to the bridge where he stood, and they gathered around. One engineer from Mumbai, and nine Deck, Engine and Galley ratings—some from Gujarat and some from Ratnagiri in Maharashtra. Ten tired men wondering why on earth they had been summoned in the middle of the night.

'Friends,' he addressed them in Hindi, trying to control the thumping of his heart. 'Do you realise what we're all doing here? We're carrying out a criminal activity which can put us in jail for ten years or more in our dirty, rotten prisons. In some countries, we'll get the death sentence for dealing in drugs. And for what? For the morsels that this ship-owner pays us? Is it worth it to risk our lives for this? Do you know that the Iranian will make hundreds of crores of rupees for this consignment? And what will we get? Just our measly salaries! Maybe a small bonus if he is feeling generous. And, God forbid, if even one packet is short at the port of discharge, we're not going to see our families again, you can be sure of that.'

He paused, breathing hard. He had their attention. They were staring at him, listening. Waiting to see where this will lead.

'But I have a plan, my friends,' Tiwari continued. The crew looked at each other uneasily and focussed their attention on their captain again.

'I have my contacts in India, and I just spoke to them. They are very, very interested in this consignment. They have promised to pay twenty lakh rupees to each of you. Twenty lakh rupees! They were not willing to dole out this much, but I convinced them. We have to deliver this consignment at Alang in the Gulf of Khambat, Gujarat. You've heard of Alang, one of the biggest ship breaking yards in the world? Well, that's where we'll go, not to Egypt.

'We're going to beach this rust bucket. She's junk anyway. Before the yard workers break her into little parts, my client's labour force will board and collect the full consignment. They'll pay us and it's over. We'll walk away into the night, far richer than we were.'

There was silence all around. Weathered, tough men weighing their chances, making their choices in their heads.

'How many of you still want to go to Egypt?' Tiwari asked them after a pause, when he realised there were no questions.

Nobody answered or raised his hand.

Tiwari hid his elation, smiled and said, 'Good! You won't regret this, friends. We will all be rich soon!' What he conveniently forgot to mention to the rest was that his promised share would be twenty crore rupees, almost USD three million. An unimaginably huge sum for a poor little boy from Chhapra, Bihar—now living in a dingy neighbourhood in north Kolkata with his wife Sangeeta, brother and parents. The prospect of that amount of wealth made him feel giddy. He could start a new life anywhere in the country.

'What about our voyage orders to go to Egypt? Won't the owner be upset? He may be tracking the vessel,' the engineer spoke up.

Tiwari dramatically walked up to the electronic panel near the radar and started hitting the vessel's Automatic Identification System (AIS) till the unit was in ruins. Then he disconnected the ship's satellite phone, rendering it powerless. Hasan Ahmadi could now try all he wanted, but would no longer be able to track the ship's location. Nobody now could.

'Satisfied?' Tiwari asked the engineer coldly, sounding more confident than he felt. The engineer nodded his acquiescence. The crew straggled off the bridge, muttering to each other, all having agreed to the proposal.

M.V.Julie set course for the Gulf of Khambat, Gujarat on India's west coast. Delighted that things were going according to plan, Tiwari picked up the satellite phone, reconnected it and made a few calls again to give his contacts in India an update. His first call was to a Vikas Yadav in Mumbai.

'Everything under control, Vikas *bhai*,' he reported with a smile. 'We're heading for Alang now. I've spoken to my crew. All are on board with the plan; no more hurdles in the way. Should reach in less than three days from now.'

'That's good to hear, Tiwari *Ji*. I'll make arrangements at my end; not much time left. You did say fifteen hundred kilos?'

'I did, trust me! Ha, ha! Er...my twenty is *pucca,* no? And don't forget my ten crew members!'

'I did promise that, Tiwari. Not a problem. That quantity should fetch a fine price through my channels, a fine price indeed.' Tiwari knew the drug dealer meant a price of about two hundred crore rupees, or about thirty-two million USD. He also knew that the contraband would be sold through Vikas' *hawala* channels in Chhapra and Sealdah in Bengal at the current rate of about INR thirteen lakh a kilo for pure white heroin.

He and Vikas went back a long way. Both hailed from Chhapra and chased their dreams relentlessly to come to the bright lights and promises of the big cities. Vikas settled into petty crime and later into narcotics to carve a career for himself, while Rajan took the more conventional sea route. But they remained in touch.

Tiwari's next call was to an Asif Merchant in Bhavnagar, Gujarat. This was an acquaintance Vikas had introduced him to a year ago. Merchant ran his own shipbreaking business at Alang, fifty kilometres from the port of Bhavnagar.

Shipbreaking is just what it sounds like. Piece by piece, workers use basic tools to dismantle ships that are too old or too costly to maintain. Recycling steel from ships like this one is a multimillion dollar industry. Merchant was not only a successful businessman with political clout, he was also known to turn a blind eye to any nefarious activity that might take place when one of his ships was being dismantled. For a small slice of the pie, of course.

Tiwari fixed his vessel with Merchant to be beached at short notice, ready for the hammers and drills and the gas cutters of the ship breaker's large labour force. This whole operation had to be done quickly before any government authority got wind of it, and sent their inspectors to investigate.

'Asif *bhai,* not more than one day at anchor for the formalities, please. I need to beach the ship as soon as possible, and start the breaking. You'll be well looked after for this.'

'*Arre,* you're talking like a big ship-owner now, not a seaman, Tiwari,' Merchant remarked with a laugh. 'But don't worry. I'll get it done.' Tiwari thanked him and hung up. He knew Vikas would have promised Merchant adequate compensation for his cooperation.

Tiwari's last call that night was to his brother Ramesh in Kolkata. He quietly and quickly gave his younger brother a synopsis of his plan and the recent phone conversations he'd just had.

'But *bhaiyya,* are you sure that...?'

'Shut up and listen,' Tiwari interrupted him, 'Buy a ticket for the next flight to Mumbai. Collect the token amount from Vikas; I've already spoken to him about it and he's agreed to pay. Then fly to Bhavnagar and wait for me there. I'll meet you in a couple of days. You'll remain in Bhavnagar and be my eyes and ears there to see that nobody double crosses me. That'll keep you close to the yard in Alang. Tell no one about this at home—not our parents, not Sangeeta—nobody! Is that clear? Just head for Mumbai, okay?' He hung up to Ramesh's bewildered protestations. He disconnected the satellite phone, this time with no intention of using it again.

Rajan Tiwari did not sleep much that night. The choppy seas and the rain squalls from the south west in the Arabian Sea did not help either. Eleven seamen tossed and turned in their bunks during what remained of that night, and not just because of the fury of the monsoon. The next day arrived to continuing rough weather and passing showers, but the ship maintained course for the coast of Gujarat ahead.

A day passed, and the ship trudged on at barely seven to eight knots, rolling and pitching to the beam swell. That night in his cabin Tiwari again went over his plan, and wondered what could go wrong. He trusted his childhood friend Vikas Yadav, but Asif Merchant he didn't know so well. However, he knew Vikas could take care of Merchant if things went awry. Vikas could be ruthless if required.

Another sleepless night passed for the young captain. On the following day the sky was clearer and the winds had died down a little. *M.V.Julie* remained on course and picked up a little speed. They would reach Indian shores that night, all going well, and would start skirting the Indian coast from Porbandar southward. His plan was to quietly sail past Diu into the Gulf of Khambat, and drop anchor off Alang by the third afternoon. Hasan Ahmadi, the ship's owner and drug lord, would be none the wiser, thinking his ship was still making her way in rough seas slowly towards the Gulf of Aden on her way to Egypt. He checked his mobile phone, and noticed that it was already picking a signal. But he refrained from making any more calls.

By dusk, the vessel was less than a hundred miles from Porbandar, on course, when the lookout on duty spotted an aircraft approaching from the east. It flew overhead and headed back towards shore.

The lookout on duty called the Captain in his cabin and reported it. Feeling a little uneasy, Tiwari came up to the bridge. On looking all around through binoculars, he saw nothing in the distance except a couple of fishing boats, lazily adrift. Yet he had a sinking feeling that something was wrong. He didn't return to his cabin, but waited on the bridge.

His misgivings proved correct when after about twenty minutes, he spotted through the binoculars two fast ships on the horizon approaching him from the direction of Porbandar. A helicopter hovered over them, also heading in his direction.

Tiwari shouted to the lookout to take the wheel, ordered helm to turn the ship right around in the opposite direction to seaward, and increased engine speed to the maximum. But it was an exercise in futility. The two Indian Coast Guard vessels gradually gained on him and were soon abreast of the little freighter, one on each side.

'This is the Indian Coast Guard ship *Samudra Pavak*. Stop your vessel immediately!' came a booming voice on a loudhailer from the ship on the right. The helicopter hovered over for a while, then turned and headed back to base. Its job was done, the two Coast Guard ships would take over. The ship flanking the left inched closer. There were armed men in lifejackets standing on deck on both vessels, waiting to board the freighter.

It was over.

A resounding slap on the side of his head woke him up, and he realised he had dozed off during the interrogation. He was so exhausted by the lack of sleep over the past three days that he was having difficulty in remembering how he got here. Tiwari realised he was in a harshly lit, windowless room with several officials sitting across the table from him.

'You fell asleep,' the lead interrogator admonished him with a sneer, 'before we could get properly introduced, my friend.' His tone was mocking. An elderly man with his hair and moustache dyed black, he introduced the others across the table. Tiwari was too fatigued to remember any name, just that they were from different governmental agencies—Intelligence, Gujarat ATS, police, Customs, Narcotics, Coast Guard and the Indian Navy.

'Where am I?' Tiwari asked, not really sure. The disorientation was making his head swim.

'Porbandar. All eleven of you. Your ship is also here. And you will all remain here till we get some answers.'

'How did you...?'

There was a ripple of laughter in the room from the others.

'How did we? Phone chatter, my friend! You talked too much! We picked up the conversations on your satellite phone. Do you think we sleep on the job just because we work in Government? The NTRO—National Technical Research Organisation—intercepted your conversations,' the lead interrogator explained.

'We don't take any chances now, Captain Tiwari,' a man in naval uniform spoke up. 'Not after Mumbai on 26/11, and not after New Year's Eve in 2014, when that explosives-laden Pakistani boat had blown itself up in the sea. How could we be sure that you were not terrorists? That you were carrying only drugs?'

'Your phone chats sent off alarm bells all over! A crisis centre was set up in Delhi and intelligence officials from twelve locations in Gujarat and three analysts, who had worked on the 26/11 Mumbai attack case, were tasked for the job,' the lead interrogator explained.

'Over twenty hours, a Coast Guard Dornier aircraft conducted a sea-air coordinated search with two helicopters and two vessels, finally accosting you a hundred miles off Porbandar,' added another officer in uniform, probably from the Coast Guard.

'What could I do, Sir?' Tiwari lied desperately, his world falling apart. 'We had not been paid our salaries. We were forced by circumstances to resort to this. How else to feed our families, Sir?'

The officials looked at him sceptically. This was the biggest narcotics haul in the country since any of them could remember, and they were not falling for a sob story.

'Hmmm...okay, now you must sing. Who are your accomplices besides the ones we know? Who all do you know remotely connected with this? In India and outside? We already have Vikas Yadav and Asif Merchant. Your brother is in Lalbazar Police Station as we speak. Kolkata Police caught him before he could take that flight to Mumbai. We can get your wife and parents there too in a jiffy, if you like. You'd better tell us more. Tell us everything.' When Tiwari just stared at him uncomprehendingly, the lead interrogator walked around the table and gave him another stinging slap on his cheek. 'Sing!' he commanded.

The thought of his ageing parents and pregnant wife in a police station was the last straw. He sang. They listened, and took notes.

Back in his cell, Rajan Tiwari lay down on his mattress and closed his eyes. How could he have been so stupid and used the satellite phone for so many calls? He felt a void in his head, a black hole, slowly swallowing all the hopes and dreams he had harboured all these years. The nothingness and the absurdity of his existence made him start sobbing quietly in self-pity. Never in his dreams had he imagined that he would end up like this—reaching for the stars, but tripping and falling into darkness.

A week later, a Maruti Ciaz car with government number plates halted outside a small house in a crowded neighbourhood in Ratnagiri town. A man in a safari suit and dark glasses was seen entering the house, coming out fifteen minutes later and driving away. Speculation was rife among curious neighbours why that important looking stranger would visit the family of Abdul Wagle, a seaman who had brought disgrace to the neighbourhood by being caught in a drug bust ten days ago and was now in a Porbandar jail—an event highly publicised by local TV channels.

'Maybe he was the one who tipped off the authorities for a reward,' someone suggested, 'and the family is being looked after while he does some time in jail?' There were some nods, some shrugs. Nobody could say for sure.

8

Transition

Keenan watched the sea, lost in the rhythmic percussion of waves on the water. His eyes gazed steadily at the horizon, young face aglow with the last rays of the setting sun. As a large, looming figure approached him, he turned to see who it was and flashed him a delighted smile.

'Hi *Grampa,* I was just thinking of you. I'm getting bored. There's nobody my age around. You got to tell me a story. *Please!'*

'I came to say bye, kiddo. I've got to go, it's getting late. Your grandma's told me not to take too long, or else...and you know she's scary when she's annoyed.'

'Yes, *Grampa*! But tell me a story first. About your sea adventures!'

'Keenu, you know your dad doesn't like me telling you my sea stories,' Capt. Oswald D'souza remarked, with a twinkle in his eye.

'Oh, Dad is so boring, *Grampa*! Please, please, please tell me one!'

The old man chuckled, nodding in agreement with his grandson's opinion of his son-in-law Savio, and sat down in the deck chair next to Keenan's. The annual family reunion at Baga Beach was drawing to a close. The relatives were all packing up and getting ready to go home. Oswald, not really in a hurry to get back, looked out at a distant ship on the horizon and let out a nostalgic sigh. The breeze blew in from the sea bringing him the kiss of a mermaid.

The boy was the apple of his eye and the feeling was mutual. He raised a gnarled hand to touch the boy's cheek.

The eleven year old gazed at the tattoo on the leathery skin of his grandfather's forearm; perhaps of some long lost love at some long forgotten port. He wondered if he would ever get to hear that one.

Keenan loved his septuagenarian grandfather—his *Grampa*—from the faded scars on his hands, old as erosions, to the brown blotches on his skin from too much sun, to the eyes that were kind, cheerful and undefeated. The occasional whiff of alcohol from the old man's breath did not faze him at all. He loved his grandfather's stories, for they were all well marinated with liberal potions of the kind of love and adventure his parents never talked to him about. The stories transported him to places he feared he would never get to see.

'Hmmph…drinks like a fish, swears like a fishmonger!' was his mother's constant refrain, making no secret of her disapproval of the old sea dog. She had seen over the years her father, as he aged, turning into a garrulous, foul-mouthed drunkard. She did not realise that it broke her father's heart to see the disappointment in her eyes, but he did his best to mask it. Her husband disliked the old man for the same reasons, but Oswald didn't care too much about what his son-in-law thought of him. Nonetheless, Erica Fernandes was also aware that her son and her father adored each other, and did not want to spoil that relationship.

'What kind of story do you want to hear, Keenu?'

'About the sea, *Grampa*! How you sailed across the ocean, what kind of work you did, the funny songs you and the other sailors sang….'

'Songs, too? You don't want to hear those. All bloody dirty songs….'

'No, I want to, *Grampa*. Please!'

It was not that the Ancient Mariner needed any further goading. In his sunset years, a captive audience and a full glass of whisky were all that he desired. Mottled fingers fondly caressing his belly, he leaned back, belched and began.

'It was sometime in '69 when I was working on an oil tanker. I wasn't a Captain then, just a junior Deck Officer. We sailed out of Venezuela after having loaded at two ports there. Three days each at Punta Cardon and Puerto La Cruz—that's another story for you, Keenu!' The old man winked and chuckled. 'But when you're older,' he added hastily.

He thinks I'm still a kid, the boy thought hiding a grin, but remained silent, waiting for his grandfather to continue.

'We sailed from Venezuela, not sure where we were heading. Just east across the Atlantic, no specific voyage orders. It still happens on oil tankers nowadays, you know, just tramping around. So there we were in the Atlantic with just the sun, moon and stars for company, kiddo. Days and weeks with nothing to see but the horizon.'

'But you didn't get lost?'

'No, Keenu,' the Ancient Mariner replied emphatically. 'We were real navigators those days! The same sun, moon and stars we had for company would help us find our way. We used the sextant those days to work out our position from the heavenly bodies in the sky. You know, by spherical trigonometry using pen, paper and nautical tables?'

'But what if it was rainy or stormy? No sun or moon?'

'Aha...good question, kiddo—you'll make a good sailor. We still managed! I told you—we were real navigators then! Not the GPS generation of today, where everything is handed to you on a platter by satellites and computers. We would stand on the bridge wing and smell rain in the air, look at the seagulls to sense land was near, notice the change in colour of the water to know that the depths below were changing. Our senses were honed razor sharp, our observation skills were high. We'd lick our finger and hold it high to find the direction of the wind at night. No bloody fancy gadgets and computers!'

'What about the songs, *Grampa,* the songs you sailors used to sing those days?'

The Ancient Mariner chuckled, 'No, no, you don't wanna hear those....'

'Come on, *Grampa,* I'm not a kid anymore! Last time you promised....'

'Okay, okay. The Brits taught us most of these sailor songs. Passed down from generation to generation. I learnt 'em as a cadet. Songs we would sing when we were bored, or drunk, or homesick, or whatever. Do you really want to hear 'em?'

Keenan waited, looking at his grandfather in frustration. Was he going to sing or not?

'Okay, okay...here goes. This one's called "Nothing Else To Do",' the old man cleared his throat and began softly, so as not to attract Erica's notice and bring her storming to the scene. He preferred facing a cyclone at sea to his daughter's wrath.

'Friggin' on the rigging, Shagging on the lagging, Masturbating on the plating, Nothing else to do!'

The boy giggled.

'You know what these words mean, don't you, Keenu?'

Keenan nodded. 'But nowadays we call it "jerking off", *Grampa,*' he replied with a straight face.

The old man looked at his grandson sharply, wondering if his leg was being pulled. But the boy's large, innocent eyes revealed nothing. The Ancient Mariner continued to the next verse, and the next.

'Another song, *Grampa*? Please!'

'This one's called "The Good Ship Venus".' The old man winked at his grandson and began a little louder, throwing caution to the winds.

There was another giggle from the boy when it was over. The old man, now in full flow and really beginning to enjoy himself, began yet another sea shanty.

The lesson in classic nautical poetry was interrupted by someone clearing her throat from behind. Loudly. The boy turned to see his mother standing behind them glaring down at him. The old man did not need to turn around to face his daughter. As he anticipated, Erica walked around to face them and remarked, trying her best to keep her voice neutral, 'Everything okay here? Keenan, you have school tomorrow and homework to do. We must go now.' She must have overheard everything, Oswald realised ruefully.

'Just a few minutes more, Mom! *Grampa* is finishing a story.'

'No, Keenan! Get up now! We are leaving,' Erica's eyes flashed fire.

The boy reluctantly got up, flashed a resentful look at her, bent down to kiss his grandfather on the cheek and walked away to collect his belongings.

'I heard everything, Dad.' Erica's voice was quiet and menacing. She stood looking down at him with her hands on her hips. *Just like her mother* was the thought that crossed Oswald's mind. Both mother and daughter were confrontational, aggressive and won every argument that had ever taken place with him. He never stood a chance, ever.

'What stories were you telling him? What were you trying to teach him?' Erica demanded to know.

Oswald tried to put on a brave front, hoping to bluster his way out of this one. But his alcohol-sodden mind struggled for a retort.

'Huh? What do you mean, Erica? The boy wanted to hear some sea stories, that's all!' The words fluttered and flew in the wind, ignored.

'You know exactly what I mean, Dad. I'm so disappointed in you!' Erica said icily and stormed off, before her father could think of a reply.

The sun was already dipping behind the horizon, but daylight still lingered in the air. The tide was coming in. The Ancient Mariner got up from his deck chair, the creak of age in his bones. He shuffled across to where the thinning crowd of relatives still remained, all waiting to get into their cars and drive away. After cursory goodbyes and half-hearted hugs, they were all gone. All except Keenan, standing dejected by himself next to his car, waiting for his parents still some distance away on the beach having a serious discussion with each other.

The old man walked across to the boy and put a hand on his shoulder.

'Whew! That was unpleasant. No more poetry lessons, kiddo.'

The boy brightened and grinned. 'Okay *Grampa*. Another one later, maybe? That one about Diana showing her legs? But tell me, how did you pass your time at sea those days?'

There in the fading light on a Goan beach, the old man and the boy, separated by six decades but conjoined by a mutual love, kept talking. The Ancient Mariner regaled his grandson with sea yarns from the 'good old days'. About the time when seamen were *shipmates*, not colleagues. About friendships that formed standing the test of time, not end at the gangway. About socialising daily after dinner, the common rooms abuzz with activity. About having an open bar, with card and chess games going on, fun and laughter and nobody caring if you smoked or not. About Saturdays being Movie Night, when the white screen would fill up with light and sound as the movie began to the whirring sound of a projector. About working long and hard hours on the deck and in the Engine Room, but not making a big deal about it; no long procedures, no fancy paper work; just getting the bloody job done. And above all, surviving to tell the tale.

As it grew dark, the old man then talked of snail mail. The joy of receiving a letter from a loved one and reading it for the first time, then the second and then the twentieth—keeping it under one's pillow and sniffing at the letter paper to remind one of that person. The joy of a lipstick-smeared, perfumed sheet of paper from one's sweetheart or fiancée, the joy of receiving a sketch or two or a scrawling 'I love you, Papa' from one's child who had just begun to learn to write....

'I still have the first letter your mom wrote me, you know that?'

It was hard for Keenan to imagine his mother as a seven year old, and he didn't want to spend too much time doing that. 'But that voyage, *Grampa*? What happened on that voyage?'

'Aaah...that voyage. We were perhaps a week at sea when hit by a hurricane. You know all the hurricanes were named after women those days, don't you?'

The boy nodded, grinning. 'So what was this one called, *Grampa*? Erica?'

They both laughed at that, and high-fived each other. 'Yes, kiddo. It may well have been. She was quite a hurricane, that one! Took us by surprise. One day, calm sea, sunny sky. The next morning, we were being tossed about like a bloody paper boat!'

The old man's eyes narrowed as he recalled that particular storm.

'The sky had turned dark and there were streaks of lightning. The wind was howling and whistling through the steel doors. The spray stung our faces if any of us ventured out on to the bridge wing. Grey-green coloured waves taller than the ship would rise before our eyes and crash down upon us. The ship rolled violently from side to side and pitched up and down. The gigantic swell of the waves would hit the ship every now and then causing her to shudder.'

Keenan closed his eyes, trying to picture the stormy seas in his mind's eye.

'This went on for a couple of days, but it seemed like a lifetime. We just hung on to our furniture and belongings from crashing down or falling to the floor.

'Then the storm passed. We were lost. We had no idea where we were. Two–three days of battling a storm in overcast conditions—God knew how many hundreds of miles the wind and sea had taken us away from our course.'

'And then?'

'Then we saw an island. Our calculations told us that it could be São Tomé, off West Africa.'

'And...?'

'Well, we approached as close as we could and dropped anchor. Our communications equipment was destroyed. We needed supplies. We lowered a lifeboat to the water, kiddo. We cast off from the ship, started the engine and headed for the shore.'

'Get in the car, Keenan,' Erica said firmly. His parents had reached the car. Keenan's face fell. The Fernandes family muttered goodbye, and drove away, leaving Capt. Oswald D'Souza to find his own way home with an unfinished tale on his lips.

'Keenan, have you completed your homework?' Capt. Savio Fernandes' high-pitched voice jolted the boy from his reverie. He disapproved of his son spending too much time dreaming. It was already 9 pm.

'Yes, Daddy,' Keenan lied. His mind was on that lifeboat heading for the mysterious island, with his *Grampa* as a young man in charge of the team.

'Then you'd better go to bed. You have school tomorrow.'

'Yes, Daddy.'

Savio Fernandes was a tense, hyperactive man in his late thirties, reluctant to waste precious minutes of his life. So much to do, and so little time! Back from the beach, he had showered and was now sipping green tea for its antioxidants and nutrients. He too was a ship's Captain, and had married the daughter of one. Ambitious and hardworking, he had gotten his promotions early in life and had already become a Master five years ago, among the first in his batch to get command of a merchant ship. But he had other plans. To him being a Captain at sea was just a stepping stone to bigger things. He wanted to become a chartering manager or a marine superintendent in a shipping company, and later move on further up in the corporate world. Truly a Modern Mariner.

'Daddy, will you please tell me a story? About your sea adventures?'

Savio scrolled down the mails on his iPhone at lightning speed. No emails to reply to from his office, his tax consultant or his Mutual Fund adviser, he noted with a trace of disappointment. 'Eh, what? Story, Keenan? No, I don't have stories to tell about the sea. Didn't your *Grampa* spin some yarns this afternoon? Your mom wasn't very happy about all the things he tells you, I can assure you. Moreover, you mustn't believe everything your *Grampa* tells you.'

The boy continued undaunted. 'But *Grampa* was a ship's Captain and you also are one. You sail all over the world and visit so many countries, like he used to. You must have had some interesting experiences too.'

'But I don't have fancy stories to tell you, Keenan. I just do my job and come home. Don't have time to waste for other stuff.'

Reluctantly, however, he left the living room with his son to put him to bed. As Keenan settled down in bed,

Savio quietly checked for any new WhatsApp messages on his phone. Satisfied that there were no pending messages requiring his attention, he sat down on the side of the bed, determined to devote the next fifteen minutes of his time to his son. Quality time with family was important, he remembered from the self-help primers he occasionally read.

'So, son,' he said, with forced cheer. 'What do you want to talk about?'

'Your sea adventures, Daddy. Do you still navigate on the high seas with the help of the sun, moon and stars?'

Savio chuckled and shook his head. 'Ha ha...not anymore! The old timers used to do it decades ago. Technology has come a long way, son. The times have changed. The ship's exact position is constantly on a graphic computer screen and digitally on several other devices all the time. We have every kind of information that we need staring at us on computer screens. Who needs the sun, moon and stars?'

The boy looked puzzled. 'So anyone can navigate the ship, Daddy, and find the ship's position? What about smelling rain in the air? Sensing a storm is coming? Or that land is close by? Taking visual bearings of other ships to see if there is a risk of collision? Do you still do these things?'

'Hmmm... I see your grandpa has been telling you what a great navigator he was, eh? Why go looking for a storm? It's simple—we subscribe to a Weather Routing Service and follow their advice. We avoid the really rough sea areas.' Savio hastily added, 'Oh, of course I did experience a cyclone in a simulator exercise during training.' He rolled his eyes. 'Pretty rough!'

Disappointment passed over the boy's face like a shadow. 'But Daddy, what about lifeboats? You must be taking your lifeboats out to the beach when you are at anchor, no?'

His father looked uncomfortable. 'No way, Keenan. There have been several accidents while lowering lifeboats before. We just have a short lifeboat drill every three months, that's good enough for us.'

'But, Daddy, *Grampa* said that if everybody....'

'Your *Grampa* says a lot of things, Keenan,' retorted Savio sharply. 'But times have changed.'

'What about the work on deck, Daddy? Like cleaning the cargo tanks on oil tankers?'

'Oh, that is not safe, son,' Savio replied. 'Many seamen have died of asphyxiation in these enclosed spaces. Nowadays we have to follow procedures.'

Smug with the comfort of his own professional knowledge, the Modern Mariner launched into a detailed lecture on the procedures for entering enclosed spaces to the eleven year old. He talked of Permit to Work, filling a Risk Assessment Form running into several pages, testing of gas and oxygen levels in the tank, appointing supervisors. He spoke of toolbox meetings and on-site review of the Permit. He talked of the special equipment to be worn by the workers going in and the rescue equipment to be kept ready outside.

The boy didn't understand much of this jargon. All he gleaned was that the actual work had not really begun. Puzzled, he asked, 'So, when do they actually go in and do some work?'

Savio looked at his son sharply, wondering if his leg was being pulled. But the boy's large, innocent eyes revealed nothing.

'Daddy, do you have fun with the other guys in the evenings at sea? Like party and all?'

'Well, not really,' Savio replied, a touch defensive. 'Who wants to, when we have the Internet? Seafarers are rarely seen after dinner. Mostly they hurry back to their cabins, toothpicks in their mouths, to be reunited with their laptops, tablets or mobile phones. The Recreation Rooms are empty. They prefer their own virtual worlds now.'

'*Grampa* mentioned the crew getting letters from home when they came to port after a long voyage, Daddy. That used to be a big day in their lives.'

'Letters? Who needs letters? We have Wi-Fi on board now. Skype and WhatsApp and Viber at our fingertips.'

The boy's eyes stung with tears of disappointment and frustration. He remained silent for a while, then burst out.

'*But it's so sad!* Sea life sounds so boring now! What about the great stories and movies made on the sea? Where are the giant whales and beautiful mermaids and one-eyed pirates and singing sirens and shipwrecks and storms and lost treasures and crew mutinies and sea songs? The sea's the same, isn't it? That hasn't changed! Then where are they? Where is the fun, where is the adventure at sea now? Where, Daddy? *Some things should never change!*'

His father stared at him dumbfounded, taken aback at the outburst. The boy calmed down somewhat, turned away and hoarsely mumbled, 'I'm sleepy now, Daddy. Good night.'

Sheepishly, the Modern Mariner stood up and wondered for an instant what he could do to assuage his son's disappointment. 'Times have changed, son,' he repeated softly and helplessly. 'It's called transition.' He waited till the boy sailed across the dark oceans of sleep to dream of things that should never change. Only then did he quietly leave the room, clicking the door shut.

9

Smoke on the Water

You know, seamen have the knack of looking out of place in any surrounding when they are not on a ship. That is how I spotted him among a sea of white Caucasian faces in the transit lounge of Zurich International Airport at Gate 12, while waiting for the last leg of my journey to Tenerife in the Canary Islands. Another dishevelled young Indian like yours truly, in a shabby jacket, dirty sports shoes and faded jeans, sporting three days of stubble, sleep deprived, clutching an inexpensive bulging backpack, fidgeting uncomfortably, apparently taking the same flight as mine.

This must be the Third Engineer Mishra that the Office had told me about, I guessed. He was supposed to have flown in to Zurich from Lucknow via Delhi to join the same ship, while I had flown in from Mumbai. We made eye contact, and gave each other a nod and a smile. In the parallel universe of seafarers, two inhabitants had yet again recognised their own among the scores of aliens present.

'Hello, I'm Manoj Singh, Electrical Officer,' I walked up and introduced myself to my countryman.

'Atul Mishra, Third Engineer,' he stood up to shake my hand with a friendly smile. He was a little taller, a little bulkier and seemed a little shier. We both sat down next to each other waiting for the boarding announcement.

'Joining *Trader 1* at Tenerife?' I asked, just to be sure, switching over to Hindi.

He nodded, and spoke in Hinglish, the language that most educated Indians seek comfort in. 'Yes, joining this company for the first time. I'm from OMI, actually. But promotions are too slow there, I got fed up. These guys at the office promised to promote me to Second Engineer within the next couple of months on this ship itself.' I refrained from commenting on his career decision.

We had to sit apart on the flight to Tenerife South Airport, but resumed our conversation in the local agent's taxi on the way to the hotel. During a walk around the pretty little town before dark and at dinner in the hotel restaurant, we got better acquainted. Being of similar age and coming from a similar North Indian middle-class background, I discovered we had a lot in common. Like a fascination for Bollywood movies and songs. Over a drink before dinner we went into raptures over the dance duet by Aishwarya Rai and Madhuri Dixit in the recent blockbuster *Devdas*.

Like me, Atul too was single but engaged to be married to Sudha, a girl from his hometown Lucknow. An alliance arranged by his parents. He had met the girl just once, but that was enough for him to have agreed instantly. When he showed me her photograph that he kept in his wallet, I could see why. I retired to my hotel room that night with the warm, comfortable feeling that it looked like Atul and I were going to be good friends, and hopefully remain so even after parting ways when our tours of duty on that ship ended.

We were informed by the local agent who called us in the morning that the ship had arrived as scheduled. It was a fine day. By 9 am, we were headed out from the pier in a service boat to the anchorage, where I got my first glimpse of the ship.

My heart sank, for the *Trader 1* was a dismal sight. The hull and superstructure were coated with rust. The gangway creaked and groaned as we made our way up, not sure if the wires on which it was suspended would take our weight. As both of us reached the deck, we put down our bags to catch our breath and looked around what would be our new home for the next few months. It was not a welcoming sight. A 'rust bucket', in sailor-speak. We looked at each other with trepidation with the same unspoken query in our eyes—if the deck and superstructure were like this, what would the Engine Room be like?

We entered the accommodation. The corridors were dank and unlit with tube lights not working in several places. The cabins were small and frugal, offering minimum comfort. On a quick round of the Engine Room with the off-signing Electrical Officer and Third Engineer, our worst fears were confirmed. The Engine Room, where we would be spending almost all our working hours during our tenure, was like a dungeon. Patches of poor lighting revealed various machineries leaking oil, guard railings broken or missing, crew ratings walking about in filthy overalls with no protective gear, steps slippery on the various ladders. Accidents waiting to happen in every corner of that vast space.

Our predecessors bid us a hasty farewell and rushed to catch the same boat ashore. I did not blame them for their haste, and pondered gloomily over having to spend the next six months in a hell-hole like this. Life wasn't fair.

Across the Engine Room, from near the boiler, Atul Mishra made eye contact with me and shrugged his shoulders helplessly. His eyes and expression said it all: *What the hell is this?*

The ship completed her bunkering operations by the next morning, weighed anchor and sailed for Marseille, a port in France on the Mediterranean coast. Over the next twenty-four hours, as we sailed for the Strait of Gibraltar, I familiarised myself with the ship and my shipmates.

Having worked in this shipping company before, I knew what to expect. Certainly no great expectations. The *Trader 1* was a medium-sized bulk carrier loaded with fertiliser. Built in 1982, she was already twenty years old. To say she was poorly maintained would be an understatement. The officers and crew were all Indian, which was good and bad. Good because I relished only Indian cuisine. No beef steaks, pork chops and boiled vegetables for me. Bad because…well, you can guess what happens when there are too many Indians in one congested place. Politics, squabbling, arguments!

The other silver lining was Third Engineer Atul Mishra, who was gradually becoming a friend. You know, there are certain people who you click with instantly, and Atul seemed to be one of them. Though I was now settled in Mumbai, I had grown up in Lucknow—studied at La Martinière College there—and the city of my childhood was a growing bond between the two of us.

On the day we sailed from Tenerife, Atul started keeping watch in the Engine Room. It was from midnight to 4 am and from noon to 4 pm, as was customary for his rank. Being an old ship with very little automation working, it was deemed necessary to man the engine spaces round the clock by a qualified engineer and an assistant.

After dinner that day, Atul voiced his fears to me, '*Batti Saab*, this ship is a disaster waiting to happen. I shouldn't have joined this outfit.'

I knew this confession would have come sooner than later, and assured him, 'Don't worry, *Teen Saab*. It's going to be alright. I know all the company vessels are like this one, but I've survived, see? And you will too. Just keep yourself busy and six months will pass before you know it.'

Atul was not convinced. '*Arre bhai, l*ook at the condition of this ship! How can you work like this? Every piece of machinery is on the verge of breaking down! There is no preventive maintenance at all—only crisis management! Today the Heavy Oil Purifier broke down. What's going to break down tomorrow? And I can slip and break a leg anywhere, there are so many oil leakages!

'And have you noticed the crew? They know nothing! They're poorly trained, reluctant to work—*ekdum* useless! The Chief Engineer seems least bothered.'

Six months. It seemed like an eternity looming ahead.

I knew that Atul was correct, but the conditions really didn't bother me that much. I had low expectations and that worked for me. To be employed was good enough for yours truly. My parents had given me an excellent education. Had I studied further and passed certain entrance exams, I would have been a Chief Engineer by now. Or in middle management in a corporate setup. But let's not go there; I have no regrets. I was not unhappy doing what I was doing. I deftly changed the subject to our hometown Lucknow. Atul brightened up and began to talk of Sudha, his fiancée. That was that.

The next day also turned out a fine day. The ship remained en route at a steady 11 knots. Atul came down to the Engine Room a little before noon after a hasty light lunch to take over his watch. We exchanged a smile and a nod—conversation was impossible amid the noise of the machinery. I was about to leave to go upstairs, when it happened.

I smelled smoke. I halted at the companionway and turned back. My heart skipped a beat, for looking down at the cavernous space where the massive main engine with its cylinder heads stared back at me; I saw black smoke billowing out into the heated air. It was gradually intensifying and filling up the entire Engine Room space. I could discern hot, black oil falling from above on to the hot surface of a turbocharger, which was running at full speed.

Pandemonium broke out, but some of us stood stunned. 'FIRE! FIRE!' somebody shouted. Some ran helter-skelter. Nobody seemed to know where the emergency escape was. The smoke rapidly became thick, so thick that it was now difficult to see anything. I remembered the location of the companionway to the upper decks and headed in that direction. In the smoke, to my horror, I caught a brief glimpse of Atul heading in the opposite direction.

'*Teen Saab*!' I called out to the Third Engineer, but Atul did not hear me in his panic, and disappeared into the smoke. The remainder of the crew trapped inside the Engine Room, more familiar with the layout, pushed past me shouting and headed for the nearest escape. I followed them instinctively.

Lungs aching for fresh air, we reached the upper deck corridor and rushed out on to the deck outside. The fire alarm had been triggered automatically and was blaring all over the ship. An announcement came over the speakers, 'Fire in the Engine Room! Fire in the Engine Room! Muster on deck! Muster on deck!'

The fire was now spreading into the accommodation. How could it happen so fast? The officers and crew from all departments were stumbling out onto the open deck. Thick black clouds of smoke choked the air. I looked frantically around among the sea of faces. Atul was missing. I started calling out to anyone who would listen, 'Third Engineer is missing! Where is Third Engineer?' Nobody was listening.

Nobody was taking charge. Nobody was taking any action to fight the fire.

As we stood on the deck in a motley group waiting for instructions, the Third Officer came down from the bridge deck with a full plastic shopping bag, the contents of which he spilled out on the deck amid the crew assembled. To our surprise, we realised that it was our passports and Seaman's Identity Books that were lying on the deck.

'Captain says manage your own documents!' the young officer announced and rushed back to where he came from, before he could be collared and attacked. There was a scramble for the booklets and a scuffle broke out. I too joined the panicked crew, retrieved my passport and my Seaman's ID Book and put them in the breast pocket of my overalls. It looked like the Captain was not taking command of the situation, and it was every man for himself. I fervently hoped I was wrong.

Someone broke away from the group and tried to rush back into the accommodation to retrieve his precious belongings. The heavy metal door for entry into the accommodation was hot to touch, but throwing caution to the winds, he tried to pull it open. There were shrieks and shouts from the rest of the crew as the door opened. There was a flash of scorching flame and a fireball whooshed out. I ran up behind that idiot and pushed the hot metal door shut, scalding my palms in the process. I rushed to the nearest fire hydrant on deck and opened it. A trickle of sea water from the hydrant cooled my hand a little. A pity nobody had started the fire pump while it had been accessible; we could have started hosing down the compartments. But it was obvious that the crew had no training for handling emergencies. Nor did the senior officers appear to be in control.

The flames were rushing out from the ship's funnel now. There was smoke coming from inside the accommodation through minute openings at the sides of the closed portholes and doors. I was certain my cabin would burn down to a crisp. It was dreadfully apparent that the fire was spreading its tentacles to destroy the whole ship.

Someone had the presence of mind to take a head count to see who was missing. I then remembered and screamed to anyone who would listen, 'Where is the Third Engineer? Has anyone seen him?' Everyone was accounted for, including those on the bridge. Everyone except Third Engineer Atul Mishra. Nobody seemed to know where he was. I recalled my last sight of Atul in the Engine Room, rushing through the dense smoke in the wrong direction.

The engine had stopped by now and the vessel had started drifting. Whether it had been stopped remotely by cutting off fuel supply, or had burnt to molten metal, I did not know. All I knew from the talk around me was that the CO_2 fire extinguishing system did not activate to extinguish the fire in the Engine Room, and soon the whole ship would burn down. I began to murmur a prayer.

The Chief Officer, the senior officer present who had finally taken charge, tried to lower the lifeboat on one side, then the other. There was no success. Years of neglect had rendered them immovable.

The end was drawing near, I feared. A young seaman started sobbing in quiet desperation. Had the Captain sent out a distress signal, I wondered? The Chief Officer, who had had the sense to bring a handheld radio with him when he escaped from the accommodation, checked with the

Captain on the bridge. Yes, a Mayday had been sent out to all ships in the vicinity, and a Distress Alert to the nearest Coast Radio Station, to everyone's immense relief.

There was nothing to do now but wait. We had no means to fight the fire blazing in the innards of the ship. Nobody could re-enter the Engine Room or the Fire Control Station in the accommodation to start the fire pump for water in the fire main. By now the fire pump located in the nether region of the machinery spaces may have already melted to a lump of metal, I feared. The fire held its head up regally as its destruction spread. It seemed to glower at the surroundings, daring them to challenge its awesome power. A subtle shift in the wind direction brought noxious smoke and ash from the funnel raining down into our hair and eyes.

I remembered my missing shipmate again. I went up to the Chief Officer, and collared him, 'Where is the Third Engineer? We have to find him!' Chief Officer Mandeep Singh brushed me aside. 'Who's going to go inside the fire to look for him? You?' His tone was contemptuous. True…rushing into the fire would be suicidal. Nobody in their panic had thought of bringing protective fire suits or breathing apparatus outside from the Fire Control Station. A poorly trained crew on a badly maintained ship had done everything wrong, and was now helpless. We would all have to jump in the water one by one to save ourselves, only to meet our watery graves, if help did not arrive soon.

We watched the glowing embers leap and twirl in a fiery dance, twinkling like stars in the hot swirling air before cascading down from the funnel and accommodation. The colour of the superstructure was slowly turning from rusty white to a charred black.

Several hours passed, while we waited and waited, adrift in the Atlantic. The sun set in the distance, causing our haggard faces to glow with its last orange rays before twilight beckoned the stars. As the fire raged on, I wondered why help was taking so long. We were surely not far from civilisation. Somebody mentioned that we were only about a hundred nautical miles from Gibraltar. Not far at all.

Eight hours later—but it seemed far longer than that; it had grown dark by then—we watched the lights of two large tugs approaching the ship from the north-east.

A cheer went up among the crew. As the tugs drew nearer, we noticed that these were Offshore Supply Vessels or OSVs, designed for firefighting. After a brief exchange with the Captain on the VHF radiotelephone, each OSV went on either side of the disabled ship, bathed her in harsh bright light from their own searchlights, and commenced hosing down the ship from both sides, with powerful jets of water from fire turrets.

Getting drenched by the onslaught of four powerful jets of water, two from each OSV, did not dampen our spirits. The jets started cooling and dousing the flames in the accommodation and the entire aft section of the ship. To us it was like being immersed in the holy waters of the Ganges, an answer to our prayers, a rescue from certain death. The fire fought back magnificently, enjoying the battle, its flames leaping in excitement, crackling and hissing like cornered animals. It took more than six hours for the firefighting OSV's to win the battle. Mission accomplished, they bid goodbye to the Captain and crew and wished us luck before departing from the scene.

'Now what?' somebody asked, as their lights receded into the distance.

'We are getting a tow tomorrow,' Chief Officer Mandeep assured the hapless crew. 'We'll be towed to a port of refuge.' I wondered if he was just saying it to make us feel better. The Captain had not yet come down to talk to us.

We huddled on deck in a corner, drenched, some of us shivering, and waited. It was a clear moonlit night. In the glow, the ship looked like a derelict, a ghost ship lost at sea under the stars that speckled in the heavens above. The inhabitants of the ship remained on the deck, none of us venturing inside the inky black darkness of the accommodation where our cabins once stood, and we waited for daybreak. The lights of passing ships in the distance comforted us somewhat. We found suitable nooks on the deck, curled up and fell into an exhausted sleep one by one.

I woke up in the morning as the sunrays glowed orange on my eyelids. As I sat up and looked around, I recalled the horrific events of the previous day with a shudder. I then remembered with a start the missing Third Engineer, and raised a hue and cry. The remaining crew members who were still dozing all woke up and realised to their horror where they were.

Two search parties were organised, one to enter the accommodation and the other the Engine Room. We felt the metal bulkheads first to confirm if these were hot to touch, which would indicate the presence of a fire still smouldering behind them inside. But, thankfully, these bulkheads were not even warm. We entered and began our search. Once inside, we broke up in pairs and scattered to cover all the areas in the labyrinths of the Engine Room and accommodation of the large vessel.

Black dust hung in the air and invaded my lungs as my partner, the Oiler, and I found the body at the Engine Room

Boiler Platform. Atul Mishra had not been able to escape the fire. Nor the pain it had caused, and the dreams it had stolen. He was barely recognisable. One arm was lying a foot away. His flesh had turned black. The sight and smell made me throw up, and I ran up to summon help.

We carried his body into the Provision Store anteroom and lay it there, covering it with the remains of a bedsheet. After that, the crew went around the entire accommodation and Engine Room to inspect the extent of damage. I checked my own cabin first. As I had feared, everything had been destroyed by the fire, except a small bag of personal effects, which included a framed picture each of God Shiva and Shirdi Sai Baba. If you don't believe in miracles, explain that.

We were called to muster on the bridge, surprisingly the one place in the accommodation that had not been damaged by the fire. It looked that the OSVs had arrived in the nick of time. The Captain, who had spent the last twenty-four hours there, looked as haggard and drawn as the rest of us. We were told he wanted to brief us on the situation. About time, I thought.

'Gentlemen,' he addressed the entire crew in Hindi, 'It is indeed unfortunate that such an event has taken place. We have lost one of our own. But help is on the way. I have managed to inform all parties concerned, and briefed them on our situation. We have no electrical power. Our Emergency Generator is not working; the Chief Engineer reports….'

I doubted if it ever did, and stealthily stole a murderous glance at my Departmental Head the Chief Engineer, who stared stonily ahead.

The Captain continued, 'We have to wait. We have no power for our engine, steering, other machinery or even lights. Our cabins are burnt, we cannot stay in them. We may have to sleep on the deck tonight as well, if help does not arrive soon. I want you to be brave and cooperate. I am hopeful a tug will come latest by tomorrow and tow us to the nearest port. We will have to discharge this cargo first, and then proceed to dry-dock for major repairs. Don't worry—*sab theek ho jaayega!'* He dismissed us with a wave and a wan smile.

It was futile to bemoan our fate; we needed to eat. The charred black surfaces of the galley along with the melted wires and appliances there told us that nothing could be cooked there. So we took some pots and pans, salvaged some dry provisions and carried everything to the poop deck aft. Wood was collected from some wooden pallets lying around and a fire was started. The two cooks managed to cook some rice and dal, just enough to feed us twenty-four survivors. Three crew members opened the Fresh water tank manhole in the Steering Gear Compartment and withdrew several buckets of water for drinking and washing afterward. When all was done, we resumed the wait. One by one we lay down on the deck in shady nooks, and drifted off to a fitful sleep. The ship continued to drift without power, left to the mercy of the wind and ocean currents. Mandeep organised lookout duties in shifts. Another long night arrived, stayed and passed slowly.

The lookout spotted the rescue tug first at the crack of dawn. It was less than a mile away. 'There it is!' he yelled in glee. Never had the contours of a squat, black tug looked so heavenly. The Captain from the bridge wing shouted to the crew below to make fast the tug on the bow. Nobody needed to be told a second time. We all rushed to the forecastle of the ship. The tug approached the bow slowly.

It took two hours, but it was finally made fast. We first threw down a thin coil of rope called a heaving line to the tug, and pulled up a thicker messenger rope which the tug crew tied to our heaving line. The messenger was tied to a really thick steel wire rope, which all of us heaved up, huffing and puffing, despite our failing strength. We put the eye of the tow rope on to a bollard. We were exhausted by the time the arrangement was completed. The tug began to pull on the tow rope slowly. We moved away as the steel rope became taut. The ship started moving at last, gradually gained momentum and started tailing the rescue tug at a slow pace.

We were finally on our way to a port of refuge.

'And then?' Her tone was playful.

'And then? We were towed to Marseille where we discharged the entire cargo into barges that were made fast alongside our ship. Took a long, long time. Then we were towed to Setubal in Portugal for major repairs in dry-dock. I left the ship as soon as I could and never returned to that shipping line.'

'And after that?'

'*Ufff...h*ow many times do you want to hear the same story for the past fifteen years, my love? I've lost count of the number!'

'As many times as I want. Please!'

I sighed and continued, 'When I got off the ship, I went to Lucknow after a few days at home to pay my respects to Atul Mishra's parents and his fiancée... I don't know why, but I just felt responsible somehow. I had grown fond of him in just those three--four days that I had known him. We would have become fast friends for sure.'

'And then?'

'And then I met you.'

'Yes. And you started coming to Lucknow every week.'

I grinned nodding, saying nothing.

'Good decision, Manoj *Ji,*' Sudha ruffled my greying hair affectionately and smiled, 'otherwise how else would we have met? Some things are destined to be....'

10

Stairway to Heaven

He came up the gangway slowly, balancing a small suitcase in one hand and a large, weathered kitbag on his shoulder. Nobody helped him, and he didn't seem to care. On reaching the deck, he looked Jay straight in the eye, flashed him a grin and stuck out his hand. There was no trace of exertion, just the sweat dampening his brow and shirtfront from that humid Madras afternoon of March 1979. Wiry, bright-eyed with a mop of hair falling over his forehead. Jay could not help liking the young man's cheerful demeanour.

'Hi! I'm Chow—the new Third Mate,' he announced.

'Chow?' Jay queried disdainfully, eager to establish his seniority over the newcomer. After all he was the Second Mate of the ship, having earned two stripes on his shoulder epaulettes, whereas this new-kid-on-the-block was just a lowly one-striper. The fact that they had the same qualifications having cleared the same professional exam was immaterial. Besides sea experience, Jay also had ship seniority over him, which meant that he had been on the ship longer than Chow had, having joined a month earlier. That counted for a lot in those days.

'It's Ajoy Chaudhuri actually. But everyone calls me Chow,' the newcomer explained, flashing another grin.

'Jay Pandit,' Jay introduced himself stiffly, still playing his 'senior' card and asked the Able Bodied Seaman on duty to take the new officer to his cabin upstairs on the Officers' Deck. The new arrival would have to meet the current Third Mate, who was going home on vacation, and spend a couple of hours taking over his duties, and familiarising himself with the ship. They were due to sail in a few hours.

Jay thought no more about Chow as he was on duty and on deck. Port Watch, as it's called and a particularly busy watch on that day. They had just completed their loading of general cargo and were getting ready to sail. The gang of dock workers left the ship, straggling in ones and twos. The cargo holds were battened down; the ship's derricks were lowered and secured for sea. The controls on the bridge were tested and the engines were made ready. All hands on board were accounted for, a quick search for stowaways yielded no unwelcome guests and they were ready to sail from the port of Madras. A little later, a harbour pilot boarded to take the ship out of the port. The mooring ropes were cast off from the jetty and picked up on board. The ship left her berth and made her way slowly out of the harbour. While approaching the harbour exit, the tugs that were assisting the large vessel hooted, signalling for the crew to release them, which the crew did. Just before the harbour exit, the pilot got off into his cutter. The ship maintained a steady heading to sail past the breakwater. She began to roll gently to the swell in the open sea, and gradually picked up speed.

It was evening by the time Jay entered his cabin, exhausted after his particularly gruelling six-hour watch, which on that day combined cargo and navigational duties. He popped open a can of chilled beer and lit up a cigarette, just to unwind and relax awhile before heading downstairs for dinner.

He had just put on some of his favourite music on his cassette recorder and his feet up on the table in front of him, when there was a knock on the door. A mop of hair followed by a pair of bright brown eyes peeped in.

'Can I come in?' Chow asked him.

Jay nodded warily. He wanted to be alone for a while, but didn't want to appear rude. At least not on the first day.

'Just wanted to borrow some cigarettes,' the new Third Mate said sheepishly. 'The Bond Store is still closed.' That same quick grin, as he stood by the door after shutting it behind him. Jay stretched forward lazily to pick up his packet of State Express 555 to toss over to the visitor, when Chow remarked, 'Aaah... Leonard Cohen, I see.' Jay's hand remained suspended in mid-air for an instant.

Leonard Cohen—Canadian poet, songwriter, singer, author. A man Jay had grown to love and worship. He prided himself on his eclectic taste in music and books, looking down on the hoi polloi with their conventional tastes and lack of 'cool quotient'. In the six years of his sea career, he had yet to find a shipmate of any nationality who had a taste in music and the finer things in life remotely resembling his. Indians generally loved Kishore Kumar, Mohammed Rafi, Lata Mangeshkar and the like...yes, he listened to them too. You couldn't possibly live in India and be oblivious to Bollywood film music. Those who considered themselves really cool claimed to like Abba, the Bee Gees and Boney M. Jay considered it beneath his dignity to admit that he even listened to pop and disco, though he did. A couple of his batch-mates used to listen to the hard rock of Led Zeppelin, Black Sabbath and Deep Purple when they were cadets at the maritime academy, as did some of the East European officers he had sailed with. Fine with him...too noisy for his taste, though. But to each his own.

But Leonard Cohen? Leonard Cohen was his, and his alone. A part of his secret world. Jay didn't know anyone at sea who had heard of Cohen. Now here was this stranger—on a cargo ship in the Bay of Bengal—mentioning Cohen's name and trespassing into his secret kingdom. Intrigued, Jay put down his feet from the table, sat up straight and offered the visitor a chair. Chow came and sat down, accepted the offer of a cigarette and lit up.

Neither spoke. They just smoked silently while the Voice of God (as Jay liked to call it) filled the cabin. Mesmerising, enchanting. A deep, mellow voice singing of life and death, joy and sorrow. Singing of yesterday, today and tomorrow. Singing of love, sacred and love, forbidden. The Master of erotic despair. Just an acoustic guitar in the background. Phrases and metaphors bringing vivid images to life in that dark room.

The cassette tape clicked loudly to a stop after about twenty minutes, ending their trance.

'Wow! That was great!' Chow exclaimed, breaking the silence.

Jay, pleased, flashed him a rare smile, stood up and they both went down for dinner.

On the voyage to east Africa across the Indian Ocean, they became friends. Chow kept the 8 to 12 sea watch morning and night, while Jay was on from noon to 4 and midnight to 4. It was only in the evenings when they were both off duty that they would get to meet and relax. Their cabins, adjacent to each other, were open house for anyone who wanted to walk in. And some did—Gus the Radio Officer and Vish the Junior Engineer would invariably be found sprawled on the sofa in one of these two cabins. All young men in their early twenties with similar ideas and dreams, seeking their own kind for company and fun.

Jay found to his delight that it was not just a love for Leonard Cohen that he shared with his new friend. They both liked progressive and bluesy rock, like The Moody Blues and Jethro Tull, immensely. They both loved reading the same kind of fiction, and they both wanted to fall head over heels in love with a girl before marrying her. It had to be love, they declared vehemently, and to hell with family name, caste, religion, race, colour and creed. Vish, or Vishwanath, on the other hand—a Tamil Brahmin—was adamant about an arranged marriage with a girl of his parents' choice. He had to bear the brunt of their ridicule. Gus, or Gustav, the good Catholic boy from Mazagon, Bombay, would quietly nod, laugh and agree with both sides. Gus had made fence-sitting an art form.

Both Second Mate and Third Mate detested their immediate superior, the Chief Mate, a pot-bellied, sly character from Kanpur who would try his best to make their lives miserable. But they had each other for support, and the tacit support of the Captain, an elderly, quiet father figure recently retired from the Indian Navy, who did not appear to like Pot Belly much either. The days passed smoothly.

Jay had found a soulmate. Chow was fun loving, carefree and good company. Off duty, they would spend all their free time together listening to their own kind of music with the lights off, or reading or chatting. Chow kept a journal with him, and would keep jotting away now and then in it. He showed it to Jay a couple of times. It was filled with scribblings—of a lost love, dreams unfulfilled, poems—a potpourri of thoughts and ideas. Jay started one too.

The vessel's first port of call was at Port Victoria in the Indian Ocean archipelago of Seychelles. Both friends along with Gus and the Deck Cadet grabbed the opportunity to go ashore in the afternoon. It was at dusk that the town of Port Victoria came to life—girls of all shapes and colours came out of nowhere. The Creole girls were a delicious shade of milky coffee. Cars and dune buggies drove by, carrying mostly white, half-naked tourists. Having got their fill of eye candy, they were heading back to their ship when it started raining. They broke into a run on the last stretch of the road to the dock gate but got thoroughly soaked. Chow, panicking because he was so late for his watch, broke all kinds of records and remained in the lead. Jay, huffing and puffing, followed and the other two trailed behind. They reached the ship gasping for air, and could hardly climb the steps of the gangway, much to the amusement of the eyewitnesses on board. But it had been fun.

A month passed on the east African coast as the ship touched ports in Kenya, Tanzania and Mozambique. Long stays in port involved discharging of textiles and cotton-piece goods from India, and back-loading coffee, cashew nuts, cloves and sisal products. Short voyages between nearby ports on the African coast kept them busy. It was not often that the two could go ashore together, given their duty hours. Yet, they somehow managed to get cheated out of all the Kenyan shillings in their pockets by two wily hookers in a Mombasa hotel room. They also nearly came to blows at the bar of the Mission to Seafarers in Dar es Salaam, over an attractive lady who was bestowing equal attention to both of them, without any actual favours.

That month passed quickly, and the ship finally sailed from Beira, her last African port of call to head back east for Sri Lanka's shores. The southwest monsoon was still a month away, and the weather was good all over the Indian Ocean.

One night on that passage, Jay's intercom phone rang at 11 pm, rousing him from his sleep. This was unusual—the Second Mate on any ship is normally called at 11.45 pm to come up on bridge for his watch at midnight. Sensing something was amiss, Jay was immediately alert and picked up the phone.

'Yes?'

It was Chow. 'Can you come up now? It's urgent!'

Wondering what on earth could be the matter, Jay quickly washed up and went up to the bridge. Chow wasn't in the wheelhouse. Jay took a moment to get his eyes adjusted to the darkness and strode out into the open to the port bridge wing.

It was a beautiful moonlit night. There was a bed sheet spread out on the deck. On it lay arranged in silent majesty, a bottle of whisky, cold water, a big bottle of chilled Coke, glasses, a cassette player and plenty of music cassettes. A picnic had been arranged on that lovely night, with the full moon glowing right overhead, encased by a shimmering halo. The whole sky glowed with a soft lustre. There was a cool breeze blowing. The flat sea stretched in all directions, the moonlight scattering diamonds across its surface.

There in the middle of the Indian Ocean en route from Beira to Colombo, the Officers of the Watch were going to have a moonlight picnic on the bridge.

'You bloody idiot!' Jay said to Chow, aghast, 'What if the Old Man comes up?'

'He's come and gone—taken his round. Never comes back. Don't worry,' Chow said confidently, and grinned. They both burst out giggling.

Keen to make it a real party, they woke up poor Gus. He came in his pyjamas and stood there politely listening to the Abba cassette that was put on, wondering when he ought to say that he was going back to bed. Chow was already certified as a lunatic by everybody on board. Jay suspected that he too was being considered one. Vish too came up on being called. They plopped down on the bed sheet, gleaming white in the moonlight, and basked in the glow of the moon. Desultory conversation over a drink ranged from the crowd on board, to past experiences on other ships, to star constellations, to women and sex, to movies, to music—the usual talk of seafarers worldwide through the ages. After about thirty minutes, Vish and Gus excused themselves and left for bed.

The two friends just lay down on the bed sheet and relaxed, looking up at the silvery moon all aglow, the starry sky and felt the gentle breeze blowing over them. Music began to take a deeper meaning. Leonard Cohen hypnotised them yet again. They talked of his books, his songs, his voice and each of them narrated when and how they had first come across this idol of theirs, while the acoustic guitar and the Voice of God listened to their conversation.

The AB on duty would come and peek at them from time to time looking worried, but he was ignored. He was an avuncular, elderly man quite fond of the two lads.

They stood up after a while to look at the masts in front of them on the deck. There was a row of Samson Posts ahead of them, resembling football goalposts, only much, much taller and stouter, between the cargo holds, right till the forecastle. The two looked at them for some time, swaying gently with each roll of the ship as if in slow motion. There was no ship in sight; just a clear, midnight blue horizon. Then Chow remarked, 'Why not go up on top of the mast? It'll be *some* experience!'

That did it—the seed was sown. They made up their minds, shaking their heads in disbelief and laughing at their own madness at the same time. Jay wasn't really high—just one or two pegs old, but was feeling just a wee bit reckless. And the beauty of the surroundings did it. They just *had* to go on top of the masts and feel what it was like to be up there. That was about 2.45 am; Jay's navigational watch had already begun at midnight. Chow went down and brought a piece of wire with which he made a sling to carry the cassette recorder. They were ready.

Jay told the aghast Duty AB of their intentions and the two left the bridge. They reached the main deck below and walked past the side of the cargo hold to the bottom of the nearest mast, in front of Cargo Hold#4. The mast towered above them. Undeterred, they began a slow, careful climb to the top with Jay leading. It was a vertical climb holding rusted, steel rungs all the way to the top. Some of the rungs were so badly corroded that these could have come away in their hands. The strong breeze hit Jay as soon as he reached the top, causing him to lose his balance for just an instant before recovering. Chow, who was following, also reached the top and they stood side by side to catch their breath, holding a guard rail. Gazing enchanted all around them, they savoured the moment.

It was beautiful. The rippled sea encompassed them, stretching far away to a sharp horizon right around. Not a ship in sight other than their own. The sky was a little clouded and the fleecy clouds looked silvery in the moonlight. That silver disc of light high above was gazing down benevolently at the two young lunatics. The breeze felt a little cooler, a little stronger, tugging at their clothes and hair…fresh, clean, crisp.

They sat down and relaxed, putting on the cassette recorder, which Chow had carried on his shoulder. The rolling of the vessel felt more pronounced from their precarious position aloft and Jay held on to the railing. Looking down, the hatch tops and the deck seemed so far, far below. Even the bridge deck from where the ship is navigated seemed quite below their level of vision.

'So this is what God feels like every day,' Chow muttered. That made Jay laugh; he didn't know why.

The music sounded heavenly, whatever they played. Jethro Tull, Billy Joel… Chow lay down on the narrow, horizontal surface of the Samson post, closed his eyes and smiled to himself. Jay wondered for a moment what Chow could be thinking about. Even he could experience moments of *real* happiness, real freedom…feelings that he had never felt before in the past. He wished life had more moments like these to offer, and laughed in delight again. He pinched himself to keep his senses.

Chow then stood up, took off his shirt and threw it. It fluttered like a large, white handkerchief away with the wind into the water. And some dolphin went insane in the middle of the ocean. Time stood still for a while.

The magic spell was shattered by a shout from the worried Duty AB, keeping lookout on the bridge wing, to tell them that it was already 3.30 am and they had better come down.

Chow stood up to shout back something rude in protest, decided against it and gestured to Jay to climb down first. By then the ship had begun to roll to a low, longbeam swell. Jay looked down at the steel deck twenty metres below him, muttered a silent prayer and started climbing down the vertical ladder slowly, rung by rung, gripping each rung tightly and making sure he did not lose his footing. With each roll, he would stop, wait for the ship to get steady again and then continue gingerly his downward journey. It seemed to take forever. When he reached the deck below, he let out a sigh of relief and called out to Chow, 'Okay, you can come down now!'

Looking up, he saw Chow, looking tiny from his position below, begin his descent. Jay hoped his madcap friend was sober enough to undertake the journey. The wind had picked up suddenly and the rolling of the ship had increased. It disconcertingly seemed to take a life of its own. To Jay standing below, the Samson posts seemed to sway from side to side slowly like a giant metronome. Suddenly, there was a cry from above and, fifteen metres above him, Jay saw Chow hanging on for dear life with one hand. He screamed in panic.

'Hang on! Don't let go! Grab the rung with both hands!' Thankfully, Chow managed to do so. The rolling subsided gradually. When the ship steadied herself, he got both his feet on a rung.

'Don't you die on me, you bloody lunatic,' Jay muttered to himself, his heart thumping, 'or we're both finished.' He realised he was trembling and his mouth was dry.

This descent too seemed to take forever, but Chow finally reached the main deck. His forced grin indicated that he was obviously shaken by that incident. They both made their way back to the bridge silently where the ashen-faced AB awaited them, witness to the whole incident.

Fortunately the AB was a discreet man, who not only was fond of the two but also shared their dislike for the fat Chief Mate. Though generally nothing remains secret on board a ship, this foolhardy incident surprisingly did. None of them spoke about this to anyone. The recklessness of the two young officers went unnoticed by the senior management, and they got away scot free. They thanked the AB profusely, who later graciously accepted a bottle of Johnnie Walker Red Label from each of them as a token of their gratitude.

It was a night to remember. One they have not yet forgotten.

'I saw Heaven that night,' Chow remarked quietly, looking at the rain falling gently on the green lawns of the Tollygunge Club in south Kolkata, where they sat sheltered under a *shamiana*. Two weathered men in their early sixties nursing their drinks and lost in their reminiscences, celebrating their friendship of almost forty years. 'It was like I was sitting next to God.' He started humming the opening chords of a classic rock hit of the 70s, a song they were both familiar with.

'"Stairway to Heaven", eh? Luckily no rung on that vertical ladder was missing or broken…or even slippery. Otherwise it might have been an effing elevator to heaven!' Jay retorted.

'And now that my daughter is marrying that son of yours, I sincerely hope that he has not inherited your mad effing genes!' He hastened to add.

They chuckled at that and lapsed into a comfortable silence, basking in the warmth of their friendship and listening to the rhythm of the rain on the canvas above their heads.

11

Little Girl Lost

'New crew on board, Chief!' the Deck Watchman announced on the handheld radio. 'The new AB, Second Cook and Deck Cadet just arrived.'

'Okay, copied,' Chief Officer Davor Radic replied from where he stood in the Cargo Control Room. He gave a cursory glance through the porthole of the CCR which gave him a view of the main deck. He saw a group of newcomers at the head of the gangway, signing their names in the Gangway Log, registering their arrival. One of them, whose back was turned towards him, was more petite than the rest; obviously a girl, who even had a dark ponytail to show for it. Yes, the Deck Cadet from the Philippines who was expected, he guessed. Jinky Something.

'Kurac![1]*'* He muttered in his native Croatian, an expletive that to him generally covered every situation which was turning out to be not entirely to his satisfaction. What the fuck was he going to do with a girl under his wing? How would she do the strenuous work required by a cadet on deck in the hot sun or in icy winds? In the Cargo Pumproom or a ballast tank in enclosed, stifling, claustrophobic spaces? Helping the Bosun overhaul this? Assisting the Pumpman repair that? How would she keep a navigational watch at sea four hours at a stretch standing on her feet? Would she lock herself up in her cabin and stay put in bed during *'that'* time of the month? Would she get seasick the minute the seas turned choppy and not turn up for work? Would the Filipino all-male crew come sniffing around her door every night? Would the officers of other nationalities too try their luck with her?

---

[1] *Kurac:* Expletive in Croatian.

A merchant ship was no workplace for a lone, single woman. Davor firmly believed this. His mind was assailed by misgivings, never having sailed with a girl before, that too under his charge. He was well aware that being the Chief Officer of the ship, these matters became his responsibility.

He had first received the news from the Captain four days ago that a crew change at the next port was imminent, and had shrugged it off as routine. Good thing actually… crew comes, crew goes, ship continues to run, work goes on, life goes on. One set of tired, homesick seafarers get to go home; another set of broke, hungry ones get back on a ship, eager to earn their livelihood again. Win-win situation for both—the way it should be. His turn to go home would come around in a couple of months.

But when he read the names of the would-be joiners on his computer screen, he was concerned. A girl joining as Deck Cadet? A Filipina amongst fifteen-odd horny *kababayan*[2] who hadn't seen a woman over the last few months, let alone stepped on land? Would he be able to manage if the situation got out of hand? This state of affairs called for another choice expletive in Davor's considerable vocabulary of earthy expletives.

'*Pička*[3]*!*' he muttered to no-one in particular.

He drew his attention back to the large panel of gauges and alarms in front of him as he resumed monitoring cargo operations, the transfer of oil cargo from the ship's huge tanks flowing through the pipelines from ship to shore and finally to the huger shore tanks of the oil terminal where

[2] *Kababayan:* Countryman in Filipino.
[3] *Pička:* Expletive in Croatian.

his ship was moored. That required his full attention, because a mistake could prove costly.

'Good morning, Sir,' a soft, feminine voice spoke from the door, 'Cadet Jinky Aguila reporting.' He turned to look at her. She was barely five foot two, but perfectly proportioned. She filled out a tight tee shirt and jeans very well, Davor noticed. Her pale brown skin was completely flawless, and glowed with perspiration due to the heat and humidity of that sunny day. A pretty girl with a shy smile. Pretty, and yet disarmingly unaware of her prettiness.

'Good morning,' Davor replied gruffly, business-like. 'Your first ship, Cadet?'

'No, Sir, my second,' the girl replied proudly.

Davor hid a smile. 'Excellent! "Experienced" hand, eh? Now don't call me Sir. You may call me Chief. Go to your cabin, unpack and report after lunch, okay?'

'Yes, Chief.' She left to look for her cabin sheepishly.

The ship completed her cargo discharge and sailed a day later from China, heading south. Over the next week or so, while she cleared the congested waters of the South China Sea and the narrow Singapore and Malacca Straits with their dense traffic and abundance of reckless fishing boats, the crew settled into a routine that is customary for a ship at sea—navigational watches, repairs or routine maintenance on deck and in Engine Room, and paper work. Davor Radic began his navigational watches from four to eight morning and evening, plus deck work and administration from breakfast till lunch. Being responsible for the training of Deck Cadets, he gave Jinky her daily routine to follow at sea, one that would enable her to learn all aspects of a Deck Officer's job—things that she would have to be adept at when she got promoted to Third Officer in the future. The Deck Cadet's Training Programme included a bit of everything.

'You're going to report for work every morning after breakfast, Cadet,' he told her a day after sailing. 'You'll work on deck with Pumpman or Bosun—I'll specify on each day with whom, okay? After lunch, on bridge you help Second Mate with chart corrections. Evening four to eight you keep bridge watch with me. Got it?'

Jinky nodded. After a bit of hesitation, she asked, 'Are we going into piracy waters, Chief?'

'Piracy waters?' Davor looked at her, surprised. Was the girl already afraid? 'No, we don't know. At the moment, we have no orders.' Then in a reassuring tone, he added. 'Most probably to Iran or Iraq, which means entering the Arabian Gulf. No pirates there. The pirates are all lurking around in Gulf of Aden.'

The cadet blushed and then nodded again before leaving for her duties.

Jinky Aguila turned out to be a quick learner, eager to prove herself in a world of sceptical men watching and judging her every move. She was twenty, and as bright as she was pretty. She tried her best to show no fatigue, and to cope with the physical exertion as best she could. It did not take long for her to become popular among the officers and crew, and *not* for the wrong reasons. She did as she was told, made very few mistakes, spoke politely only when spoken to and kept her distance from all.

'Come here, Jinky,' Davor called out to her one evening while on watch on the bridge as he sat on the high pilot chair and gazed out into the dusk. 'Tell me more about yourself.'

She talked and Davor listened, while trying not to look at her, trying to remain impervious to her obvious charms—her perfect, smooth clear skin, the swell of her breasts, her almond-shaped eyes, pretty profile and her soft voice with the quaint accent. By gentle, probing questions he got to know more about her.

Jinky's family was not well off. Her parents had a small farm in Luzon, barely making ends meet. Her father had scrimped and saved to send her to high school. She did not let her parents down. Topping her class in high school, she had applied for and secured a scholarship to study at MAAP, the Maritime Academy of Asia and the Pacific in Bataan, Philippines—considered the top marine academy in the country. Having done very well at the Academy too, she was selected by three top shipping companies, but chose this one to launch her sea career. She didn't have a boyfriend, and was more interested in obtaining her Captain's license before contemplating marriage.

Davor got to learn more and more about her as the days went by. Small stuff like she loved Western country music, had two younger brothers she fought with and loved salmon steak.

The ship continued heading for the Arabian Gulf at slow speed, waiting for instructions on which port to proceed to for her next oil cargo, while the commercial operators ashore networked with brokers in the oil tanker market to fix her next voyage.

Davor enjoyed her company on the bridge watch every evening. He liked it best when the light of day would drain away, giving way to the velvety dark of night. It would get pitch dark in the wheelhouse, bar the faint glow emanating from the radars, ECDIS and other navigational equipment. He would then walk past her as close as possible without touching her while she stood looking down at the radar screen, her face illuminated by green glow, and he would inhale the smell of bath soap from her. She always smelt clean and sweet. If Jinky felt his presence behind her, she gave no sign. He would repeatedly fight the urge to grab her in his arms and crush her mouth with his own. The fact that there was always a Filipino lookout present on watch would cool his ardour somewhat. There was also the matter of the Company having a strict Sexual Harassment Policy, and he had no idea how Jinky would react to his advances. So, better sense prevailed throughout the voyage.

It is very easy for a seaman to fall in love. A seaman is generally lonely, love-starved and vulnerable to pretty girls on a ship at sea. Most of the time it is lust, but he doesn't know that at the time. Davor was falling for Jinky, and he didn't like it at all. He was after all a married man with a young daughter and was twelve years older than the Deck Cadet. Not the ideal condition for a new romance to blossom in his life.

No such conditions seemed to be a hindrance to Chief Engineer Manjit Singh, who suddenly developed a keen interest in navigation on that voyage, the kind of interest he had never exhibited before Jinky joined. The large, middle-aged Sikh came up to the bridge almost daily in the evenings to note the ship's position, speed and course and ask for the weather forecast. On any pretext, he would grope in the dark and never miss an opportunity to touch Jinky here and there. Not a word of apology from him; just heavy breathing. The girl would flinch, move away and suffer in stoic silence. Manjit always made sure Davor wasn't nearby, of course, for the word had already spread of the Croatian's soft corner for the girl. Nothing remains secret on a ship.

Jinky too did not report the matter. Perhaps she was afraid of the repercussions. It is a man's world, after all.

Neither did she reveal to anyone about her secret fear of pirates boarding her vessel. She had watched the Tom Hanks movie on the subject twice before coming out to sea. She read the industry manual called *BMP4,* and the weekly piracy bulletins that the office sent—whatever she could find on the subject—of Somali pirates who attacked merchant ships in the Gulf of Aden plus a large area beyond, extending well into the Arabian Sea. She would stay awake some nights, shuddering at the thought of what the pirates would do to her, being the only woman on board. But she kept her fears to herself, fearing ridicule.

The days passed routinely. Jinky worked hard, studied when she could, avoided getting too friendly with anyone on board, and was well liked by all. Davor was enchanted by her, though he tried his best not to show it. She was simple; she raised no complaints, no tantrums. If she felt unwell, she did not show it but soldiered on. It was her inner beauty that lit her eyes and softened her features, Davor thought. When she smiled, he couldn't help but smile too. When he made her laugh sometimes, she did so shyly and it was music to his ears. Davor realised he wanted her more than anything.

The voyage orders came when the ship had entered the Arabian Sea, still at slow speed to save on fuel. They were to load their next oil cargo at Marsa Bashayer, Sudan for the Far East.

'Sudan, gentlemen, means going to the Red Sea. And that means passing through the Gulf of Aden both ways and possibly saying hello to Somalian pirates!' Captain Lyakhov announced with false cheer during the morning coffee break at 10 am, when the senior officers on board would meet informally every working day. Nobody smiled.

'*Sranje*[4]!' Davor muttered, unable to hold back yet another expletive. Piracy was the scourge of his profession. Pirates off Somalia and Nigeria were hijacking merchant ships whenever they could and holding ship, crew and cargo on ransom for months, and merchant sailors could do little to protect themselves. Their lives were difficult enough without the threat of being captured, starved, beaten or killed by pirates.

The middle-aged Russian captain pretended not to hear that swearword and continued, 'Now that we have set course to the Gulf of Aden, we have two days before we enter the High Risk Area. Time to put all anti-piracy measures in place, gentlemen, before it is too late. You have until tomorrow evening to be ready.'

The senior officers after some more discussion got up and left the Conference Room, each immersed in his own thoughts and plans.

There is little a merchant ship can do to protect herself against pirates in speedboats armed with AK-47 assault rifles and rocket propelled grenades. But whatever measures needed to be taken, Davor had less than two days to get those done. These involved fitting coils of concertina razor wire around the deck's perimeter, rigging high-pressure fire hoses and water cannons aimed to blast attackers off the hull, and propping up dummies in overalls and helmet

[4] *Sranje:* Expletive in Croatian.

at the stern and on bridge wings, to suggest the presence of a watch. He had to make sure all access to Bridge and accommodation was secured to prevent these from being opened by pirates from the outside. The Chief Engineer would see to the security of the machinery spaces. Kevlar bulletproof jackets and helmets were to be placed on the bridge for protection against gunfire to the navigation team. Steel netting akin to chicken coop wire mesh had to be rigged on both port and starboard bridge wings to hopefully thwart RPGs. And so on....

The main task that Davor knew would take the longest was the rigging of the razor wire all around the main deck of the ship, as well as the different accommodation decks of the superstructure. It had to be done correctly for it to be effective. The coils of barbed wire had to be rigged overhanging from the ship's rails in a double roll, and had to be properly secured to the vessel to prevent pirates pulling them off from below with a grapnel. The work had to be unhurried, as the barbs on the wire were sharp and could cut and scratch badly. All going well, he would just about finish all the preparations by the end of tomorrow, if he started right away. The day after tomorrow they would reach the Gulf of Aden, the hotbed of piracy. The ship *had* to be ready before that. They had no other defence. Their company had not arranged for armed guards to board and sail with the ship, a practice many other companies had adopted.

It was post lunch by the time the Deck Crew organised themselves and began rigging the razor wire that day. The Bosun formed two teams, both starting from forward, one on each side of the ship. The late August sun beat down with unrestrained brutality. The crew helmets cocooned their heads in sweat; the heat licked at their sunburnt faces. The work was slow and painful, but they made steady progress. By the time the sun set, the razor wire had been rigged in circular, barbed coils right from the forecastle down port and starboard sides of the ship till the accommodation superstructure. But there was still a lot left to be done the next day.

'Continue from where you left off yesterday, Bosun,' Davor instructed Bosun Nicandro the next morning when the weather-beaten, middle-aged head of the Deck Crew reported for the day's work. 'We don't have much time. Under the lifeboats, then continue aft to the stern. Once the main deck is over, start on the accommodation decks. Even if the pirates make it to the main deck, they should not be allowed to come up to the bridge. If they do, then we're screwed!'

Bosun Nicandro nodded sceptically. Both men knew that if the armed Somalis got to the main deck, it was all over for the ship's crew. The razor wires on the companionways to the accommodation decks wouldn't be of much help then.

'Are you sure about putting wire under the lifeboats, Chief? Maybe we should keep 'em clear of any obstruction, just in case....'

'You're gonna lower lifeboats in Somali waters, Bosey? No, thank you! Just put the razor wire under them too. With a quick release arrangement,' he added. Bosun Nicandro's shrug to that remark indicated he did not agree with his superior. But orders were orders.

Jinky was aghast when she heard the news of the ship's destination. Her worst fears had come true, but she tried her best to conceal her trepidation. She, on her part, was now determined to help 'harden' the vessel with all possible anti-piracy measures so that the attackers would find it extremely difficult, if not impossible, to board. She reported on deck after breakfast to lend a hand with the razor wire.

Dressed in overalls, safety shoes and a hard hat too large for her, she looked like an adorable doll, and elicited a couple of friendly whistles and comments from the crew. When she put on her sunglasses in the bright sun on her pert little nose, Davor thought she looked like a million bucks in two dollar shades, and smiled. Resisting the urge to walk up to her and hug her tight, he turned and walked away.

'Come to help us, *Até*[5]?' The Bosun asked Jinky affectionately in Tagalog, the common language in the Philippines.

Jinky nodded.

'Well, you can start with the other guys untangling and uncoiling this wire. Then we will lay it over side along the ship's plating, okay? Be careful...the wire has sharp points sticking out!'

Jinky nodded her understanding again, her heart thumping, trying to appear calm and collected. Were they really going into pirate-infested waters?

The Bosun walked ahead to the main deck to supervise the work that had just commenced there. Along with another seaman, Jinky walked under the port side lifeboat suspended overhead, outboard of the safety railings to stand by for the wire to be passed on to her so that she could do her part of untangling the tight coils and laying them as instructed.

---

[5] *Até:* Sister in Filipino.

Two of them, both standing on the edge with just the sea rushing past about fifteen metres below....

Then Jinky was gone.

One moment she was squatting on the edge, the next moment as she stood up shakily she overbalanced. Ordinary Seaman (OS) Mendoza who was standing with his back to her barely five feet away heard the scream, whipped around to find her not there and heard the splash a second later. He caught a glimpse of her in the water, and then nothing at all. She did not resurface after that.

It took a whole, precious minute for OS Mendoza to fight his panic and the pounding of his heart to think of what to do next, before he raised the alarm on his handheld radio. He rushed to the nearest lifebuoy and threw it overboard for Jinky to grab, hoping she would see it. By now the crew on the deck were all aware of what had happened. Someone threw a wooden pallet into the sea, then another. By the time emergency procedures were activated on board, the ship had already travelled about a mile from the spot and was still moving away.

The bridge duty officer threw a lifebuoy, this one attached to a Man Overboard light and smoke marker, from the port side bridge wing. He raised the emergency alarm, bringing the Captain hurriedly up to the bridge. The ship immediately changed from autopilot to hand steering and commenced a manoeuvre to return to the original spot where the girl was last seen in the water. Additional lookouts were posted to watch out for a person afloat. Other ships in the vicinity were alerted.

But there was no sign of the girl.

Over the following three days an extensive search was conducted involving their own ship, several other vessels and search-and-rescue aircraft. There were numerous sightings of the lifebuoys and wooden pallets. But Jinky was not spotted.

Three days later the search was stopped in consultation with the local search and rescue authorities. It was over.

The ship was asked to halt at Singapore on her return voyage en route to Japan. Senior managers from the Head Office boarded there to conduct an investigation. As a result, a lot of heads rolled due to that tragic incident. The company's reputation was tarnished in shipping circles, and somebody had to pay. Based on the senior management's belief that the root cause was a lack of safety culture and that the rot started from the top, the services of Capt. Lyakhov, Chief Officer Radic, Bosun Nicandro and OS Mendoza were terminated with immediate effect.

Three reasons were given for their dismissal. Firstly, no Safe Work Permit involving overside work had been prepared. A Safe Work Permit is a document that identifies the work to be done, recognises the hazards involved and the precautions to be taken. It ensures that all hazards and precautions have been considered before work begins. Evidently, in this case, they had not. No risk assessment had been carried out and discussed with the participants. Secondly, no one had thought of wearing safety harnesses and inflatable life vests when working outside the safety rails, where there is every chance of losing one's balance and falling overboard. Last but not the least, nobody stopped the two young seamen from performing that unsafe act in an unsafe condition, when it could have saved that girl's life—that is, nobody on board stopped the crew from going outside the railings without a harness. Nobody questioned why there was no permit made, why the hazards of the job were not discussed beforehand, or if it was really necessary to rig razor wire abreast a lifeboat.

That was six months ago.

Davor Radic is nowadays seen hanging around the cafés and bars of his hometown Split, because he has plenty of time on his hands. He has been unable to get a job at sea ever since his services were terminated. The crewing agencies in town are wary of giving him an assignment. His wife has left him taking their daughter with her, due to his moody outbursts and alcoholism; he was becoming unbearable to live with. He now does part-time work operating the yachts of other owners, taking tourists out for a spin in the marina or to nearby islands.

On the days he has nothing to occupy himself with, he walks on the Adriatic seashore alone at sunset, looking back on all that he could have done right on that fateful day. If only he'd been careful, if only he'd not been in such a hurry, if only....

The guilt comes and goes...like a wave around his ankles during a rising tide. When he looks at the sky he thinks he sees Jinky, flashing that unforgettable shy smile, gazing down at him. With a shaking hand, he blows her a salty kiss, calls out her name and holds back his tears.

12

Just a Seaman

Depression settled on him like the damp of a smoggy, sunless Delhi winter day, as the taxi began its journey to the airport. Siddharth settled down in the backseat. His mother, he knew, would still be standing at the balcony and remain there till the taxi would turn the corner out of sight. Back to work, he sighed. Back to four months of isolation at sea, with twenty-three strangers from different third world countries. Back to gazing at the sea all day and all night long. Back to visiting oil terminals in various countries where shore leave was forbidden. Back to the smell of crude oil and gas that pervaded every oil tanker that he had ever worked on.

The queue at the Emirates counter for the Economy passengers at Terminal 3 of Delhi's Indira Gandhi International Airport was long. Siddharth wondered as he joined the line how many seamen like him were standing in it. The gloomier faces, he guessed, with a tinge of self-pity. As the line crept forward at an interminable pace, he whiled away his time trying to guess what each passenger in the line, all clutching passports and papers, did for a living, whether they were married, where they could be heading after Dubai and so on....

The young Sikh at the check-in counter flashed Siddharth a bright smile while reaching out to take his passport and papers. Some furious clicking at his computer, and he looked up and said, 'There, Sir! Baggage checked in all the way to Port Elizabeth, your final destination!'

'Huh? But I'm flying Dubai to Johannesburg first, boss. Then to Port Elizabeth. So the last leg is domestic, right? I think I'll need to collect my bag at Jo'burg and check in again for the domestic leg.'

Another ingratiating smile from the officer, 'Don't worry, Sir *Ji*! Your bag will be waiting for you at Port Elizabeth.'

Siddharth shrugged his acceptance, checked in his suitcase, collected his boarding passes to Dubai and Johannesburg, and walked across to clear Immigration. To join another long, snakelike queue of sleep-deprived people with passports and papers in hand, bound for somewhere....

Hemmed in by two loudly snoring passengers on the leg to Dubai, he couldn't sleep much. At Dubai airport, while killing time to take the connecting flight, he walked around the glitzy, brightly lit duty free shops cursorily, and soon had had his fill of the gold jewellery, electronics and expensive whiskies and wines that were on display. He was quietly amazed to realise that there was not a single object among the hundreds of items displayed that he needed or desired. Yet thousands of others apparently did as they thronged the shops jostling each other. His head grew heavy and his body ached to stretch out on a chair among the hundreds of seated transit passengers and drift off into blissful sleep. But there were hardly any seats available.

Sleep yet eluded him on the flight from Dubai to Johannesburg as he just about managed to squeeze his large frame into the Economy middle seat, flanked on either side by equally large Africans who were muttering their discomfort throughout the eight hour flight. The sleeplessness seeped into his pores, dousing his brain in its thick toxicity. He tried his best to doze off and probably did black out for an hour or so.

It was a bright mid-morning when the plane touched down at Johannesburg. As he cleared Immigration, he remembered that his suitcase would be transferred to the flight to Port Elizabeth by the airport staff as per the baggage tag; so he did not linger at the baggage claim area. He left the Arrival Hall and, following the signage, took the escalator to the upper floor for the Domestic Terminal. At the check-in counter, as he received his boarding pass for Port Elizabeth, he remembered to casually ask about the transfer of his suitcase. To his relief, he was rewarded with a bright smile and a thumbs-up sign from the girl across the counter, whose braces in her teeth twinkled in the light, a glaring contrast to her ebony skin.

An hour-long, bumpy ride on a small plane did nothing to make him feel comfortable, except perhaps to console him that his journey was ending at last. Before his journey across the oceans would begin. Travelling to far corners of the world to join a ship was, in Siddharth's opinion, the worst punishment God could have devised for a seaman, among a long list of punishments that He, in His divine wisdom, had already prepared for his cursed fraternity.

The plane landed roughly, swaying from side to side. Siddharth, with his heart in his mouth, waited for it to stop shrieking, slow down and come to a standstill, which it finally did. He stepped out into the bright noonday sun and walked across the tarmac, his backpack on his shoulders, along with the motley group of passengers into the Arrival Hall. They all made their way to the baggage claim area.

The conveyor belt of the baggage carousel started slowly and began steadily to disgorge luggage of all colours and shapes. These were collected by their rightful owners who walked away briskly. Siddharth kept his eyes glued to the belt for his large blue suitcase. It did not appear. It was only when he realised that he was the last man standing at the belt in a now deserted area that it dawned on him that his luggage had not arrived. His heart sank. Asking for directions, he located the airline desk for baggage claims, and filed his complaint, showing them his boarding pass and baggage tag. 'Not to worry, Sir,' the girl behind the desk told him, as she handed him a ticket. 'Probably in Jo'burg. You should have claimed it there and checked it in again.'

'But I was told....'

'It's okay, Sir. No worries. It should be here by tonight.' 'It had better be,' Siddharth thought to himself as he turned away to exit the Arrival hall to look for his agent. He cursed the attendant at Delhi airport who had glibly checked in his baggage to the wrong destination, confident in his ignorance. The thought of sailing away on a ship for the next four months with just the clothes on his back, without any of his other clothing or personal effects that he had packed for a long stint of several months, was too appalling to bear. He had just one pair of briefs and a tee-shirt in his backpack for a contingency like this, along with his laptop and documents.

He stepped out into the bright sunshine and was relieved to find a tall, sunburnt, skinny man in Bermuda shorts and dark glasses holding up a sign stating the name of his ship. Thank God there was someone to receive him, he thought. He waved in recognition and walked up to the stranger. They shook hands.

'Neil,' the agent introduced himself. On learning about Siddharth's missing bag, he grimaced. 'Oh crap! But I think it should arrive by tonight. I'm taking you to a hotel now. Your ship's already arrived, but the weather is pretty bad out in the anchorage; so there are no boat services to the ships out there. The forecast isn't that good for tomorrow as well. I'll keep you informed.'

Not in a hurry to join a ship and be cut off from the real world for months, this was the only bit of good news for Siddharth on that day. It would also give him more time for his bag to be located and shipped to Port Elizabeth. It would give him time to catch up on his sleep and even hopefully see some night life as well. How he loved night life—he just couldn't get enough of the neon lights, the pulsating rhythms of music, the dancing, the women out to have a good time, and the babble of voices…night life was what made him come alive, like a wolf on the prowl.

It was a short drive along the picturesque seashore to the Pinewood Hotel on Beach Road. As he followed the agent up the steps to the hotel entrance, he turned around. The view of the sea was spectacular. Just across the road lay the beach and beyond it the southern part of the Indian Ocean. Differing shades of blue water stretched till the horizon before his eyes. There was a cool breeze blowing in, giving him the taste and smell of the brine. South Africa was lovely, he decided.

The lobby was cool and dark. It was apparently an old three-star hotel, as he could discern from the surroundings. Unpretentious, but tidy. The unsmiling blonde woman at the front desk checked him in. He received a small piece of paper with a Wi-Fi password along with the room key.

'Excuse me, Ma'am, may I get some lunch?' he asked. 'I missed lunch because I was travelling.'

'Lunch is closed,' was the laconic reply.

'I understand. But I'm sure the hotel could arrange a sandwich for me? I've had a bad day. Been travelling in a plane all night, and now my bag is missing too.'

'Lunch is *closed*!' The lady repeated slowly, speaking as one would to a retard.

Siddharth turned in frustration to seek help from Neil, but the agent had quietly sidled away once the check-in formalities had been completed. Neil waved from outside the glass door, standing next to his car, and gesticulated that he would call when there was news. So much for the hospitality, Siddharth thought angrily. He glared at the woman, muttering an expletive in Hindi. She glared back, as he turned and walked to the elevator to go up to his room.

A visit to the bathroom and within minutes of taking off his shirt and jeans, the jet lag sucked at him like some colossal leech on his energy. He fell on the cool, inviting bed on his back. As he gazed at the ceiling, sleep came like the falling of an axe and he blacked out.

It was dark when he came to, and it took him a while to realise where he was. Switching on the bedside lamp, he looked at his watch. It was 8 pm. He washed up, and called the front desk to enquire if there were any messages for him. There were none. His stomach growled with hunger as he made his way down to the lobby. At least he'd get some dinner at the ground floor restaurant this time, he hoped.

There was nothing in the limited menu at the buffet that appealed to him. He avoided the dried, salted meats and the grilled pork sausages and settled for some spaghetti bolognaise and orange juice. Hunger satiated, he walked out to the lobby. The same woman at the front desk looked at him stonily with her hard, grey eyes. '*Bitch doesn't like me*,' was the thought that crossed his mind. Siddharth glared back and walked out into the night.

The wind had picked up, he noticed. A cool, fresh wind from the sea was driving the waves to crash on the beach beyond the road, sending white spray high in the air, which caught the light of the street lights. Savouring the fresh sea breeze placing salty kisses on his face, he decided to look for some night life. In any case, he had been told he wasn't joining the ship that night and the agent hadn't called with any change of schedule.

He left the hotel and started walking along the beachfront. Hotels, offices, restaurants... Beach Road was lively that night with moderate traffic on the roads and several couples and small groups of pedestrians passing him by in the opposite direction. The neon lights of a pub twinkled their welcome at him, right there on the beachfront. '*The Beach Shack*', the neon sign said. He walked in.

The bar was full. It was a Friday night after all. The crowd was young, college students mostly, mainly white. Dozens of conversations in loud voices, all of them competing with the rock music that thumped its beat from huge speakers at the far end of the room. Siddharth made his way through the warm bodies to the bar counter to order the local craft beer. As he waited for his chilled mug, he felt a hand on his shoulder. He turned around.

To his surprise, he saw a girl of coloured ethnic origin looking at him and smiling. His heart skipped a beat. She was beautiful. Her skin was the colour of milky coffee and flawless. Five foot seven, willowy and a face cut right from the pages of a men's magazine. Chestnut brown hair styled in an Afro, dark eyes and a dazzling smile.

'Hi! I'm Jennifer!'

'Sid,' he mumbled, and they shook hands. He couldn't believe this was happening. It was not often that beautiful girls came up to him and introduced themselves.

'Buy a girl a drink?'

'Of course! What will you have?'

Together, drinks in hand, they elbowed their way through the noisy crowd and found a place to sit outside the pub. A view of the dark sea welcomed them as the breeze ruffled their hair and cooled their faces.

They talked and drank. Drank and talked. She told him that she was studying Architecture at the local Nelson Mandela Metropolitan University and lived in a girls' hostel not far from where they sat. Her family was in Cape Town. He told her about himself, his job, his family and his hobbies. An hour or so passed before a lull in the conversation.

'Shall we get out of here?' She looked steadily at him while sipping her third Margarita.

He had lost count of the beers he had consumed. He had already told her that he was staying at the Pinewood just a short walk away. He guessed that is what she meant. Heart thumping in anticipation, he casually replied, 'Sure. My place?'

She nodded.

The night clerk at the front desk gave him a strong glare of disapproval when he noticed the girl. Siddharth ignored him while pressing the elevator button to take the girl up to his room.

They stood facing each other beside the bed in the dim light of the bed lamp. He kissed her near the mouth long and slow, she twitching her head away quickly at the last minute to avoid lip contact. Then he moved behind her. She leaned back and rested against him. He bent her forward an inch and found the tag on her zipper at the back of her neck. He eased it down, past the clasp of her bra, to the small of her back. He tipped the dress off her shoulders. It fell in a puddle around her feet.

She was warm. He bent her forward again, just an inch, and unhooked her bra. He smoothed his hands over her shoulders, pushing the straps off. The bra joined the dress. He cupped her breasts. She leaned back, turned her head and allowed him to kiss her again on the left side of her mouth. Again, a last-minute, imperceptible turn of the head. He eased her panties down. Clumsy thumbs. She stepped out of her shoes, and turned to face him. Naked, apart from the small earrings. She nodded with a slight smile. He understood. He took off his tee shirt and jeans.

She rode him like a cowgirl, facing him. Just the way he liked it. Hips thrust forward, shoulders back, head up, muttering something he could not quite follow. It was over soon. They both collapsed on the bed in a tangle of arms and legs. Within minutes, he was asleep in her arms.

A few hours later, he woke up with a start. She was gone.

Sensing something was amiss, he looked for his iPhone to check what time it was. He could not find it. Panicking, he rummaged in his jeans for his wallet. The wallet was there but empty. He checked his backpack for his other personal belongings. Those were all there. Just his phone, his cash and credit card were missing.

He cursed his folly and went downstairs to report the theft to the front desk. His outburst was met by a stony, triumphant stare from the night clerk. There was very little sympathy as he had feared. Yes, the lady in question had left an hour ago. No, he had no instructions to stop her. Yes, Siddharth would have to wait till 9 am to speak to the manager.

'But that may be too late,' Siddharth protested. 'She may skip town!'

'Well, you should have known better, Sir. You are not allowed to bring local girls into the hotel. I wanted to tell you when you entered, but did not want to make a scene. The hotel cannot be held responsible for your loss.' Another stony stare from the man made Siddharth turn away despondently.

He went back to his room and decided to wait for the senior staff to arrive in the morning. He lay down on the bed, his mind in turmoil. What a day from hell this was turning out to be! Luggage missing, no clothes, no mobile phone, no cash, no credit cards. Could things possibly get worse? Could he join a ship and live there for months without clothes to wear? In what state of mind would he be to do his job properly?

The General Manager, who met him in the lobby in the morning, was of not much help. Dave Richards smoothly put the entire blame for the incident on Siddharth himself.

'Why don't you have CCTV cameras in the public places?' Siddharth demanded.

'Don't need them, Sir. Never did.'

'I need you to call the police. Now!'

That day went by in a blur, as badly as the day before. Two police officers dropped by an hour later and took down all the details. They were quite matter-of-fact about the whole incident, and did not pass judgment on why he had brought a woman back to his hotel room. They just noted down the facts. When asked if he wanted to open a criminal case, he declined, not sure why.

Later in the day they dropped by again and asked him to accompany them to the station to identify someone. But the suspect turned out to be someone else, a black woman in her thirties. He was relieved in a way. He wanted his iPhone and money back, but he did not want the beautiful Jennifer to get thrown into jail. In his own pathetic way, he was already half in love with her. After all, he was just a seaman.

When he got back to the hotel, there was another unwelcome surprise. Neil the agent was waiting for him to take him to the ship.

'The weather forecast now says it's okay to go out to the anchorage. Ship's going to sail tonight. We have to leave.'

'But my suitcase hasn't arrived yet!' Siddharth protested.

'They're still looking in Jo'burg. Haven't found it yet. The airline will search in Dubai as well. We'll send it to your next port. Come quickly—I'll wait outside.'

Siddharth was bundled off with his backpack to the waiting car. Not before the General Manager's sneer turned into a startled look of rage when Siddharth showed him the finger on passing him in the lobby. He silently mouthed another expletive in Hindi to the front desk woman who was back at her station since morning, and received a glare in return. Neil noticed his gestures but did not comment.

The journey to the ship by boat was long and tiresome. Despite the weather not being very good, it appeared to him that the agent was in a hurry to get him on board for whatever reason. As the boat approached the rusty behemoth looming larger by the minute, Siddharth wondered what else could go wrong. Surely things couldn't get worse.

Couldn't they? The ship weighed anchor and sailed that night. Two days later, Siddharth was surprised to be summoned by the Captain to his office. He had served with the Captain before as a Third Mate and knew him to be a kind and just man. However, to his consternation, he noticed that Capt. Smith was fuming.

'What is this?' The older man demanded, handing over two sheets of paper to him.

It was an e-mail from the Port Elizabeth agent enclosing a complaint filed by the Pinewood Hotel. As Siddharth started reading the report, his blood turned cold. It was a letter written by the hotel General Manager to the agent Neil.

29 January 2017

Mr Neil Constance

Blue Flag Shipping Agency

Re: Damaged/Out of Order Room

Dear Neil,

Many thanks for calling at the hotel earlier today to view/discuss the condition of room 112 which had been occupied by one of your client's guests. Following below is a full report of the situation that occurred at the Pinewood Hotel.

It is about Client Mr Mathur, Siddharth who was an 'on-signer' to the ship Glory Bay. *The guest was booked into the hotel on the afternoon of Friday 27 January 2017 and checked out on the late afternoon of Saturday 28 January 2017.*

During the evening of Friday 27 January 2017, the guest evidently left the hotel and visited a venue called the Beach Shack. During this period he met a woman who escorted him back to the hotel. When the said woman left the hotel she left with his iPhone and wallet. The theft was reported to the hotel reception and the police were called; the gentleman did not want to open a criminal case but the police took down his details and later called at the hotel to take him to identify someone. We are not sure what the result of this identification was or if he found his mobile phone.

On the afternoon of his departure, you arrived to collect the gentleman and take him to the ship. While you waited outside for him, it was reported to me that Mr Mathur reeked of alcohol. He requested someone to carry his backpack to the vehicle, was not even prepared to lift his carry-on luggage, which although not out of line, we find very unusual. I take this opportunity to mention that he was rude and abusive to my staff in his gestures and speech on more than one occasion.

After he vacated, the housekeeper went into his room to allow the cleaners in and found that not only was the bathroom in a disgusting state but the room was also flooded. The tap in the bathtub had been left running. There were traces of blood and vomit all over. The entire bathroom area was flooded as well as the entrance hall (carpeted) and approximately half of the room which also includes water being sucked up into the wooden skirting in the affected area. A copy of the carpeting quotation will be forwarded in due course.

The unfortunate fact is that the carpet that we need to use in the room has to be shipped in from Johannesburg and cannot be laid until such time as the floor has completely dried. The second unfortunate fact is that this room now has to be removed from our saleable stock until such time as the carpet has been replaced and during this week we have two nights where we are fully booked so will now have to relocate those guests to another establishment at our expense; very bad for our reputation with clients.

At no time did this guest inform us of these mishaps, and honesty can go a long way. In our industry we put up with a lot of mischief and situations, but this has just gone too far to be ignored. The fact that you can leave a room in this condition and not even apologise is beyond comprehension.

Following below are some pictures that we took after lifting the carpet.

(There were photographs of a hotel room badly damaged by water with the soaked carpet rolled up and a wet floor.)

As stated earlier, in our industry we have to be very patient and forgiving, but there is a time when you have to take a stand and the fact that this person could not even take the time to inform us of the problems, or even try to clean up after himself, establishes that he should be held responsible and accountable for his actions.

Yours sincerely
Dave Richards
General Manager

'Well?' Capt. Smith interrupted his thoughts, his blue eyes boring into his.

Stunned, it took Siddharth a minute to gather his thoughts before bursting out, 'This is unbelievable, Sir. All lies!' He hadn't seen this coming. Were they framing him because he was rude to them?

'Well, it's your word against theirs.'

'These guys are saying that I called the bell boy to take my backpack down. If that is so, why didn't he notice the room was flooded? He would surely have reported it immediately! 'And carry on luggage? What carry on luggage? I had none!' Seven years in this Company, Sir... my record is clean!'

'Hmmm...son, I know you and like you. But I also do know that you're a horny bugger and love your drink. So I don't know what to believe.'

'But, Sir....'

'Look, Sid, seamen are scapegoats wherever they go. Easy, bloody targets. They are simple, trusting and a bit naïve in the ways of the world. Everybody takes advantage of that fact. The Head Office, the port authorities, the agents, the charterers, the Coast Guard, even the bloody ship suppliers, repair workshops, hookers, thieves...you name it. Yes, it is possible the hotel is framing you and trying to renovate one of their rooms at our company's expense. But who's going to believe you? You're just a bloody seaman.'

'But the Head Office should....'

'Who cares, man? You're just a seaman. You know seamen are treated like criminals now. Remember the tanker *Prestige* about fifteen years ago? The poor Captain was handcuffed and put behind bars for wanting to enter a port of refuge in order to save his ship. The Spanish authorities saw him as a criminal, not a hero who saved his crew and stabilised the ship when it was foundering.

'So who gives a shit about seamen, son? If it is not *convenient*,' Capt. Smith made the inverted comma sign with his fingers to emphasise the word. 'Or if it gets embarrassing, the Company will let you go. Simple as that. They don't want bad publicity.'

The Captain paused for a bit, looked at him kindly and continued in a softer tone, 'Remember, son, there is a dignity every one of us as seamen needs to uphold when we leave our country. We represent our country outside it. We are like brand ambassadors. I don't think you kept that in mind when you arrived in South Africa. You did screw up. It doesn't matter how much of this report is bullshit. Very few are going to believe you, because they'll think that there can be no smoke without fire.'

On being dismissed, Siddharth left the Captain's office, his legs like jelly, and went up to the bridge wing to be alone with his thoughts. He felt as desolate as the swell of the dark ocean thirty metres below and all around him, with nothing on the horizon except more of the same. Penniless, shirtless, soon to be jobless. In a span of two days. Just two days. How could it all happen so fast? What would he tell his mother? How easy it would be if everything went dark, and the world ended right here, right now. What a relief that would be. He prayed for a miracle to save him. But why would that happen? He asked himself ruefully. He was just a seaman.

The dark water looked enticing. That was the last thought in his mind before he jumped.

Acknowledgements

To my friend and colleague Ravindra Ramarao for giving me the ideas for so many stories, including *The Piano Man, Miss Me?* and *Reach For the Stars.* If my non-seafaring stories see the light of day, then there are many stories in that collection too for which I have to thank him. He later read the drafts of all these stories and provided valuable suggestions.

To my sister-in-law Rachel Chatterjee for patiently going through all my stories with a fine-tooth comb and editing them like a professional. She also provided fine suggestions to several for improvement. I will need to thank her for the non-seafaring stories too when the time comes.

To my brother Upamanyu who read some of these stories and offered valuable suggestions, which I have incorporated.

To Erica Fernandes, my colleague Keenan's fiancée, for the idea of *Sapphire Blue*. She too read all these stories and gave me her first impressions, which proved to be invaluable. I owe her big time for the previously mentioned 'landlubber' stories as well, when that project materialises.

To my friend and colleague Ameya Apte who gave me the idea for *The Visitor*. He is the Abhay in the story.

The Hijack is based on the real-life incident of the hijacking of the ship *Brilliante Virtuoso* obtained from various press releases online.

Reach for the Stars is also based on newspaper accounts of a real incident involving Capt. Suprit Tiwari and the ship *Hennry* that took place in 2017.

Beetashok Chatterjee
April 2019

About the Author

Beetashok Chatterjee is a ship's captain by profession. He joined the Merchant Navy at a young age and still loves it, having completed more than forty years at sea already, and still counting.

When ashore, this old sea dog lives in New Delhi, India. He is married with a son and a daughter. His hobbies include listening to Western music, reading fiction and watching cricket. He also loves good Hollywood and Bollywood movies.

Beetashok can be contacted at:

Facebook: https://www.facebook.com/beetashok.chatterjee

Twitter: @bravo_charlie1

Email: chatty05@gmail.com

Glossary of Marine Terms Used

Able Bodied Seaman (AB)	An experienced seaman in the Deck Department; above the rank of Ordinary Seaman (OS)
Accommodation	Living quarters for crew in the super-structure or erection above upper deck
Aft	At, near, or towards the back part of a ship
AIS	Automated Identification System device, part of an automatic tracking system that uses transponders on ships for identifying the ships. Used by vessel traffic services
Anteroom	Small outer room
Ballast	Sea water taken into designated tanks aboard a vessel to provide stability, especially when the ship has no cargo on board and is in a light condition
Batti Saab	Term used to address Electrical Officer among Indian crew
Beached	The process of a ship or boat being dragged ashore on to a beach, grounded deliberately for repairs or for scrapping
Berth	A term used in ports and harbours for a designated location where a vessel may be moored, usually for the purposes of loading and unloading
Boiler	A huge, closed vessel in which water is heated, and steam or vapour is generated for various purposes on board a ship
Bollard	A short, thick metal post on the deck of a ship or a quayside, to which a ship's rope may be secured

Bond Store	A storeroom on board a ship in which dutiable goods like alcohol and cigarettes are stored, for the consumption of the crew on board only; normally sealed in port by the local Customs authorities.
Bosun (Boatswain)	A Petty Officer, the senior-most crewman in the Deck Department, in charge of the Deck Crew
Bow	Forward part of a ship or boat
Breakwater	A barrier built out into the sea to protect a coast or harbour from the force of waves
Bridge	The room or platform from which the ship can be commanded; when a ship is under way, the bridge is manned by an officer of the watch aided usually by an able seaman acting as lookout
Bridge Deck	A high deck from where a ship is navigated, where the bridge is located
Bridge wing	Walkway extending outward from both sides of a pilothouse to the full width of a ship or slightly beyond, to allow bridge personnel a full view to aid in the manoeuvring of the ship; Officers use bridge wings when docking or manoeuvring in locks and narrow waterways
Bulk Carrier	A merchant ship specially designed to transport unpackaged bulk cargo, such as grains, coal, ore, and cement, in its cargo holds
Bulkhead	An upright wall within the hull of a ship
Bunkering	Refuelling a ship
Cargo Control Room (CCR)	Room or office where the loading and unloading of the ship's liquid cargo can be monitored and controlled

Cargo Hold	Vast storage space in the lower part of the interior of a ship's hull for cargo in crates, bales, etc. or unpackaged cargo in bulk
Cargo Manifest	A document listing the cargo on board for the use of Customs
Chart Table	Table located in the navigation area on which navigational charts are laid out so that the ship's positions can be plotted on the chart
Chartering	The hiring of a vessel and crew for a voyage between a load port and a discharge port, or for a time period
Charts	A nautical chart is a graphic representation of a sea area and adjacent coastal regions; nautical charts are essential tools for marine navigation
Chief Engineer	Head of the entire Marine Engineering department on the vessel and responsible for the maintenance and operation of all engineering equipment on board; has four stripes on his epaulettes
Chief Mate (Chief Officer)	Officer who heads the Deck Department and is second-in-command on a merchant marine vessel; has three stripes on his epaulettes
Chief Petty Officer	Senior non-commissioned officer
Coast Guard	A military or naval force employed in guarding a coast, or responsible for the safety, order, and operation of maritime traffic in neighbouring waters
Companionway	A stairway on a ship leading from one deck to another
Convoy	A group of ships travelling together, typically one accompanied by warships for protection

Cruiser	Type of warship
Deck Officer	Officer working in an executive department of a ship, responsible for the navigation, manoeuvring and safe handling of the ship, communications between ship and shore, the handling and delivery of cargo, and the operation of all lifesaving devices; Chief Officer, Second Officer and Third Officer are all Deck Officers
Deck Cadet	Apprentice learning to be a Deck Officer
Derrick	A lifting device composed at minimum of one pole with a pulley at the top which can be articulated over a load by adjusting its guide ropes on either side of the pole
Drydock	A large dock from which water can be pumped out; used for building ships or for repairing a ship below its waterline
ECDIS	Electronic Chart Display and Information System—is a geographic information system used for nautical navigation, has replaced paper nautical charts
Electrical Officer	Officer who is member of the Engine Department in charge of all the electrical systems on the ship
Engine Room	The space that houses the propulsion machinery of the ship, along with generators, boilers and associated machinery
Fitter	Petty Officer in the Engine Department who operates machines to produce parts or tools by turning, boring, milling, shaping, slotting, grinding or drilling metal stock or components; fits and assembles metal parts, tools or sub-assemblies, including welding or brazing parts

Forecastle	The forward part of the ship, the triangular deck area at the forward end
Freighter	A cargo ship; a merchant ship that carries cargo, goods, and materials from one port to another
Funnel	Large metal chimney on a ship from where the exhaust gases of machinery are emitted
Galley	Kitchen on a ship
Gangway	Stairs used to board or disembark ships
Grapnel	A device consisting of several metallic hooks at the end of a rope, used especially to hold fast to something
Group transit	A group of merchant ships travelling together for safety, but without armed escort (as opposed to Convoy)
Gyro Compass	A compass based on the principle of an electrically powered, fast-spinning gyroscope, used widely on ships
Hatch cover	Weathertight movable structures designed to cover cargo holds to prevent any ingress of water into the holds
Hatch top	The top surface of the hatch cover
Hull	The watertight body of a ship or boat
Kitbag	A long, cylindrical canvas bag
Knots	A knot is one nautical mile per hour (1 knot = 1.15 miles per hour)
Liberia-flagged	Ship registered in Liberia
Liferaft	A small, rigid or inflatable boat, in addition to lifeboats, carried for emergency evacuation in the event of a disaster aboard a ship; a quick release and pressure release mechanism is fitted on ships so that the canister or pump automatically inflates it, and it breaks free of the sinking vessel

Lifebuoy	A buoyant support, usually ring-shaped, that has a connecting line allowing the casualty to be pulled to the rescuer in a boat
Longshoremen	Labour force whose job is putting goods onto and taking goods off ships in a port
Lookout	A person assigned for the observation of the sea for hazards, other ships, land, etc.
Machinist	See 'Fitter'
Main Deck	The principal deck of a ship; the highest complete deck on a naval vessel extending the full length and width of the ship
Mayday	Word used around the world to make a distress call via radio communications; signals a life-threatening emergency
Messenger Rope	A rope sent ashore or to another ship to haul in an even thicker rope, for example from a tug, in order to make it fast on board
Mooring rope	A rope that secures the ship to a wharf
Nautical Mile	A unit used in measuring distances at sea, equal to 1,852 metres
Offshore Supply Vessel (OSV)	Motor vessels that regularly transport goods, supplies or equipment in support of exploration or production of offshore mineral or energy resources
Off signing	Leaving the ship to proceed on leave
Oiler	Members of the Engineering Department who help keep large ship motors and engine parts properly lubricated; they also record gauge readings, do machine repairs and perform routine maintenance and cleaning tasks

Oil tanker	A cargo ship designed to carry crude or refined oil in bulk
Ordinary Seaman (OS)	The beginning grade for a member of the Deck Department; a rank below that of Able Bodied Seaman (AB)
Outboard	Towards, or near the outside of a ship
Paint Locker	Small store for storing paint drums
Pallets	A flat wooden structure that heavy goods are put onto so that they can be moved using a fork-lift truck
Poop Deck	The aftermost deck of a ship
Port	The left-hand side of a vessel, facing forward
Porthole	A small, usually round window in the side of a ship
Pumpman	A Petty Officer in the Deck Department who tends, operates, or cares for a cargo pump and other deck maintenance, usually found on board oil tankers
Pumproom	Space, usually several decks below, on a tanker containing the cargo pumps and associated pipelines
Purifier	Centrifugal separators found in Engine Room to remove contamination from fuels and luboils
Radio Officer	Licensed officer on board a ship who handles the function of radio communications; also responsible for maintaining the radio equipment and electronic navigation equipment
Rating	Crew on board who are neither officers nor petty officers, non-commissioned sailors
Razor wire	Metal wire with sharp edges or studded with barbs, used as a barrier to deter intruders

Repeater	A navigational compass, under the control of a gyroscope
Salvage	Process of recovering a ship and its cargo after a shipwreck or other maritime casualty; may encompass towing, re-floating a vessel, or effecting repairs to a ship
Samson Posts	Structures on deck resembling a goal post supporting derricks for cargo operations
Salvors	Persons or ships participating in the voluntary rescue of a ship at sea or its cargo.
Second Cook	Assistant to the Chief Cook; usually is responsible for preparing food for the ratings and petty officers
Second Mate (Second Officer)	Licensed officer in the Deck Department subordinate to the Chief Officer but senior to the Third Officer; two stripes on his epaulettes
Second Engineer	Licensed engineer second in command to the Chief Engineer in the Engine Department; three stripes on his epaulettes
Sextant	An instrument used to measure angles; mainly used at sea to measure the altitude of heavenly bodies above the horizon to calculate the ship's position
Sign off	See 'Offsigning'
Starboard	The right-hand side of a vessel, facing forward
Statutory	Required by law
Steering Flat	The compartment containing the steering gear
Steering Gear	The machinery used for controlling the direction of a ship that allows the ship to be steered

Stern	the back part of a ship
Superstructure	The parts of a ship, other than masts and rigging, built above its hull and main deck
Supertanker	A very large oil tanker; also called 'VLCC'
Teen Saab	Third Engineer, as he is addressed among Indian sailors; two stripes on his epaulettes.
Third Mate (Third Officer)	Licensed officer in the Deck Department. Ranks below the Second Officer; one stripe on his epaulettes.
Third Engineer	Licensed engineer ranking below Second Engineer
Tug	Powerful small vessels used to tug or pull vessels that cannot move by themselves like disabled ships, oil platforms and barges, or big or loaded ships in a narrow canal or a crowded harbour
Turbocharger	A supercharger driven by a turbine powered by the engine's exhaust gases
Underwriters	Those who provide marine insurance to their ship-owner clients.
Upper Deck	A higher deck on which lifeboats are stowed
Video Data Recorder (VDR)	Collects data from the sensors on board the vessel and stores it in an externally mounted tamperproof unit called the Crash Survivable Module (CSM).
VHF radiotelephone	Signifies the very high frequency range between 156.0 and 174 MHz, inclusive; the radiotelephone is used for ship-to-ship and ship-to-shore verbal communications

Visual Bearing	Horizontal angles taken by ship's compass of land objects or other ships to determine ships' position or if risk of collision exists, as the case may be
VLCC	Very Large Crude Carrier. Also called 'Supertanker'.
Warrant Officer	Petty Officer higher in rank than enlisted personnel but lower than commissioned officers, having some technical expertise in an assigned field
Watchman	Person who is on duty or keeping watch at that time
Wheelhouse	Literally an enclosure that houses the steering wheel; the captain navigates the ship from the wheelhouse; also called 'bridge' or 'pilothouse'